Seaplane to Sounion Cove
An Ellie Pincrest Mystery

By
Devin Todd

To Agatha and Margery,
Thank you for inspiring me to write well again.

This is a work of fiction. Names, characters, businesses, places, events and incidents are either the products of the author's imagination or used in a fictitious manner. Any resemblance to actual persons, living or dead, or actual events is purely coincidental.

"If we could sell our experiences for what they cost us, we'd be millionaires."

Abigail Van Buren

*Memorial Day weekend
1986*

Chapter 1.

Boarding a seaplane

Ellie Pincrest likely would've never gotten on that seaplane if she knew one of the other passengers would be dead before the end of the long Memorial Day weekend.

As the taxi turned on to East 23rd Street and headed toward the East River where the seaplane that was about to fly her away was docked, she took a stock of herself: Her boyfriend of five years had broken up with her rather unceremoniously the Saturday before as they stood near the maître d' at his favorite restaurant. The pronouncement was so out of nowhere, so confidently, almost dispassionately, delivered that her only comment was a hazy, "Do you still tip the maître d' if we don't go in?" Her mother wasn't speaking to her for the umpteenth time in the year 1986. A Mother's Day present lacked the precision her mother, a surgeon, valued in gift wrapping. Her father was on the road 250 days out of the year as a jazz saxophonist of renown, but to make coin from his trade, he knew he had to be on the road. Ellie's job was rewarding, even enviable. She was respected, liked, pretty, and humble, so on one level she knew her life maybe wasn't all in the "Dismal" column. Though it sure didn't feel like it.

As summer of 1986 was about to commence, she realized she was three years past the age of twenty-ten. As the taxi pulled up to the dock, she felt very alone.

She had a small weekend bag that the pilot smiled at, then took from her and stowed as the seaplane gently bobbed up and down on the East River. She winced as she realized her bag was a never-used Victoria's Secret promo bag that was jammed into a corner of her closet. Her regular weekend bag was still at the apartment of her ex-boyfriend. The pilot, a sixty-something endless hippie looked her up and down and said, "Thank God you use my plane so often, looking at you gives me a reason to live." *Top Gun* had opened a few weeks before, so the pilot had changed his sunglasses from Wayfarers to Maverick-inspired Aviators.

She appreciated that he took her reservation to be on the plane on short notice; she had to get out of the city. Now.

The pilot told her to get in the co-pilot seat. She loathed getting in the seat next to him as that made her the *de facto* co-pilot and she believed his basketball hiding paunch was evidence of frequent trips to the cardiologist.

She ducked her head into the plane and saw the two back seats were already occupied with men. In the back behind the pilot's seat was a man, about her age in a three-piece Brooks Brothers pinstripe suit with slicked-back black, early-stage male pattern baldness hair, brown eyes, and a smirk. He was drinking a large Foster's lager out of a can and reading a financial report on his lap. His Rolex pointed at seven o'clock. He looked over at her and said, "Sweet!" The other man, a twentysomething, couldn't have been more different. He wore ripped jeans and a punk rock-style t-shirt that read, *STOP THE SLAUGHTER—BAN BABY OIL*. He looked up from his book *The Mammoth Hunters*, frowned and said flatly, "If we crash, you'll die first."

Dropping *A Perfect Spy* on the seat before she herself dropped awkwardly in, Ellie Pincrest looked at a sheet of dark sky far off in the horizon. A few hours ago, it had rained hard enough to get Noah's attention, but the skies had cleared and there was a brilliant blue sky on the other side of the dark sheet. With a setting sun to their right as the engine fired, they moved away from the pier.

"That thing with the engine ping, you fixed that, right?" Ellie asked the pilot nervously.

"What ping?" the pilot said absentmindedly and took the throttle up to forty percent to taxi out into the East River. As he did on every trip with his passengers, he handed over a big bag of candy and a can of Pepsi. Ellie took some butterscotch disks and handed the bag back. Sitting on the East River, the buildings of the East side of Manhattan seemed to grow taller. She was born here, raised here, knew it nuances and tricks the way old coaches knew how to win close games, but for this weekend, she was going to the place she loved, going to it in a plane almost ten years older than her.

She was off to Sounion Cove.

In a thinly-veiled nod to safety, the pilot always reached over to Ellie's seatbelt buckle and checked it in the few moments before the throttle went up to one hundred percent. He always grabbed a little bit more of Ellie than she liked, but the first time she'd taken the seaplane several years ago, she didn't have her seatbelt on and as they took off, she lunged into him almost causing a catastrophe. She'd been on the plane several dozens of times since then, but he always went for it.

"Gee," *Ripped Jeans* said from the backseat in a coquettish voice, "aren't you going to check my seat belt like that?"

The seaplane, named *Tallulah* after the actress, cut through the small waves of the East River adroitly and with a *puh-puh-puh* of the final three waves, they were airborne. The pilot, who went by "Mac" banked the plane hard left and Ellie, looking down, could see the five East River bridges: Brooklyn, Manhattan, Williamsburg, Queensboro, and Triboro. She began to feel like an escaping Indiana Jones as Jock's seaplane pulled away from the Hovitos.

"I hate snakes," she said to herself muffled by the engine noise, and she smiled for the first time since last week.

Turning her head, she looked down at the reason she always took the seaplane, the L.I.E., or Long Island Expressway, or as she liked to refer to it: *The World's Longest Parking Lot*. She used to take a bus out to Long Island, but sitting in a bus with a chemical toilet fifteen feet away became a weekly queasy festival. Her mother, who hated planes, would always say to her, "The bus isn't going high or fast enough to get you killed."

Theoretically, she could drive there, that is, if she had a driver's license, but since she'd been born and raised in Manhattan, there was no reason to get a license when she was of age. She went to college at the Rhode Island School of Design and she simply took Amtrak from the city up to Providence whenever she was home. She'd never really even considered getting her license.

And, of course, Sounion Cove didn't allow cars on Main Street. She stayed at her grandmother's house, her mother's mother's house and that was three blocks off Main Street in the largest and oldest house in Sounion Cove.

Sounion Cove is on the "South Shore" of Long Island where all Long Islanders will tell you that the beaches are better as they're on the actual Atlantic Ocean. The "North Shore" is on the more placid Long Island Sound. It's about a thirty-five minute seaplane flight, easily beating the four hour traffic-packed ride on the L.I.E. Sounion, which most people call it, was first inhabited by Greek fishermen who named it after a cape on the Attic peninsula in Greece. The Temple of Poseidon is there as is Lord Byron's inscription carved into the base of one of the columns. It's mentioned in Homer's *Odyssey* as well as by historian Herodotus.

The Long Island Sounion isn't steeped in as much history. A famous admiral was born there. Lindbergh used to land on the beach in Sounion to test landing gear back in the twenties prepping for his famous flight to Paris. Ellie's grandmother lived there as did her grandfather before he passed away in the early seventies on the fourth at Shinnecock Hills a few moments after carding an Eagle. He died happy. Ellie's mother was from there. Ellie's mother was Miss Everything at Sounion High School: Valedictorian, Captain of the State Champion Lacrosse team, most beautiful girl, and torturer of high school boys' hearts. As a high schooler, Ellie's mother swam a mile in the ocean every morning before class and local legend had it that she punched a mid-sized Thresher Shark in the snout one cold morning in September her sophomore year.

Ellie's mom went to Brown on a Lacrosse scholarship and graduated *Cum Laude* and went promptly to the medical school at Brown where she again was at the top of the class. Presently, she is the chief E.R. doctor and surgeon at one of the top hospitals in New York City. Her only child is Ellie, born on a day in which Dr. Pincrest had done rounds in the morning and wasn't about to let her water break until she was finished. And this was in the early-1950s.

Ellie's father is a Julliard-trained jazz saxophonist. He is a hard-drinking, hard-womanizing saxophonist who is, remarkably and honestly, deeply in love with his wife. Ellie's mom is familiar with the hard-drinking, not so much the hard-womanizing. Ellie is familiar with both aspects of her father's life. She's thrice run into him on the streets of Manhattan practically necking with a much younger woman as they walked down the sidewalk. Her father is very good looking, charming, ridiculously talented, and the only person on the planet Earth who can tell Ellie's mom what to do and she'll do it, no questions asked. It is almost as if Ellie's mom lives in a reality distortion zone when she gets around her husband. Several of his records have hit the top of the Jazz charts and he garners the respect of musicians and critics worldwide.

"Where do you work?" asked the Investment banker as he took a swig from the Foster's. He wordlessly offered Ellie a swig as she turned around.

"I run a design firm."

"What kind?"

"Brand identity."

"What does that mean?" He was checking out her chest and not making eye contact.

"We design logos."

"We?"

"Yes. There are thirty of us."

"Thirty? How many people need logos?"

"Who doesn't?"

"Touché. Are you the office manager or something? Is that what you mean by *run*?"

"No, I'm the President."

"Aren't you a little young?"

"The person who promoted me thought otherwise."

"Where's he?"

"In the big cemetery in Queens near LaGuardia."

"Oh, sorry."

Out of politeness (her father always told her as a young girl, "If someone asks something about you, you then ask about them.") she asked where he was an investment banker.

"How did you know I was a banker?"

"Three-piece suit in 75 degree weather, spreadsheet on your lap, Foster's at the end of the day. Rolex."

He smiled a little condescendingly. "Would I know any of the logos you've designed? Oh, wait. I should say, 'brand identified,' right?"

The smile vanished when she told him a truncated list of what she'd done. The television network one, the home appliance one, the computer one, the car one.

"Stop, Jesus. Okay, I'm impressed."

"I'm not trying to impress you."

"How long have you been president?"

"About three months."

"What happened to your boss?"

"He worked himself to death."

"Sorry." He seemed to mean it.

Ripped Jeans said, "That computer logo sucks. It just looks like a spiral. Anyone could that."

"It's unlikely," she said hoping to staunch debate.

He made a spiral motion with his hands and rolled his eyes.

"Can you describe a spiral without using your hands?" she asked.

"Of course I can," he said dismissively.

"Do it."

"It's a . . ." He used his hands.

Dangit.

"When you have . . ." He did it again.

Frick.

"A line goes . . ." And he went down swinging on strike three.

She said, "When I walked into my interview for design school, the head of the design department, this legend in the design world, in a thick Swiss accent asked, *'Describe ze zspiral without ze handz.'* I did it without hesitating and I got in." She smiled at the memory.

"Aren't you going to ask me what I do for a living?" asked *Ripped Jeans*.

"What do you do for a living?"

"Absolutely nothing," *Ripped Jeans* said sardonically.

Chapter 2.

Two in a diner

The plane skirted the shoreline all the way to Sounion, banked and came around on final. Over the years, Ellie had gotten used to being inside a plane landing on water instead of a nice firm runway. Mac the Pilot landed in the distinctive, almost circular cove, hence the name, with water as smooth as a mill pond. The plane taxied up to the dock, revved its engine and then cut out.

Ellie felt like a buzzing beehive from the engine vibration. As she got out of the plane, she saw her grandmother at the far end of the dock, looking her usual fifteen years younger than she was. To Ellie's mom's horror, twice she and her mom were mistaken for sisters. A hand grazed her butt as Ellie got out, but she didn't turn around to see which of the two from the backseat it was.

Mac the Pilot handed over her bag and asked, "Monday evening flight home?"

"Yes."

"Don't do anything I wouldn't do," he said.

Ellie walked up and hugged her grandmother. She wore very worn blue tartan plaid shorts (Ellie thought she'd been wearing the exact same shorts since Richard Nixon was first elected President.), a white linen long-sleeved shirt rolled up past her elbows, deck shoes that had holes in the big toes, an envious tan, and a huge smile.

"I heard about Stephen," she said.

"Mom?"

"Actually, your father. He called from Stockholm."

"Did he seem pleased or pissed?"

"You know your father--"

Investment banker walked up and interrupted, "Aren't you going to introduce me?"

"I haven't introduced myself," Ellie said a little annoyed at the interruption.

The banker lightly took Ellie's grandmother's hand and kissed it. "James Winnington III."

While this was happening, *Ripped Jeans* walked into town without even a glance at the three of them.

Ellie's grandmother withdrew her hand like it almost got stuck in a garbage disposal. "I bet you are."

"Lived here long?" he asked.

"My whole life. Like my mother and her mother too," Ellie's grandmother said.

"Is your last name Sounion?"

"No, but everyone's middle name here is."

"How quaint," he said with a sniff.

"And you're an undertaker?" Ellie's grandmother asked. "Did someone die in the village? Generally, I would know about it."

"No, I'm a-a-," he stammered.

"A British politician?"

"No, uh, I'm a-a-," he seemed lost

"A what? Come on, sonny. Keep up. We're time-warped villagers here, but we're sharper than most. You've come to a beach community in a three-piece suit. What gives?"

"Grandma, he's an investment banker," she said it like she got a difficult *Daily Double* question correct.

"Ahhhh," Ellie's grandmother said. "The managing partners have time parameters on when you can remove the garb?"

"No."

"Where'd you go to school, hon?" she asked.

"Hon?" he asked back. Then said, "Dartmouth," but it rhymed with *vermouth* he was so flustered.

"Fine school, fine school. And what are you doing here with no overnight bag, a briefcase, and hard shoes on mostly sandy ground?"

James Winnington III got a foothold back on the conversation and with pride and an extended square jaw, he said, "Matching up those capital have-nots with capital haves, Grams."

Ellie's grandmother, who went by "Mill," short for "Millicent" smiled at the repartee and patted him on the shoulder, "Nice comeback, but goodness knows what you mean."

The banker looked around like Alexander the Great reviewing his empire, "Yes, we mean to do some capital providing right here."

Ellie and Mill looked at each other and raised their eyebrows.

The investment banker kissed Mill's hand again and in one quick motion extracted his business card and put it in Ellie's hand. The paper was so thick and sharp, Ellie wondered if it could cut a tomato. "I never did catch your name," he said to Ellie.

"Ellie Pincrest."

Pointing at the card, he asked, "Did you do our logo?"

"No."

"More's the pity." He was back in his saddle after the quick jabs from Mill. Chest and jaw out, stomach in.

"How long are you here Mr. James Winnington III?" Mill asked.

"Dunno. Meeting someone here tonight, staying over. Don't have any clothes out here, a car, or a place to stay. No jammies even." he winked like a snake, if a snake winked.

"Are you meeting a have or a have not?"

He smiled a knowing smile, turned and walked away up toward Main Street without saying goodbye. Ellie and Mill figured the kiss on Mill's hand was the goodbye.

"Should I be frightened?" Mill asked.

"Probably. Anyone with a spread sheet and no sandals and swimwear can't be good. You didn't get a chance to answer my question, did my dad seemed pleased or pissed about Stephen?"

"Oh, your father always hated Stephen. Always told me he was a pompous ass and about a quarter as smart as you."

Bemused, Ellie said, "Dad never let on with me."

"Is my daughter still not talking to you?"

"No. I mean, yes. She is still not talking to me."

"The Great Gift Wrapping Controversy of 1986. What was the specific infraction?"

"I did a pointed corner on one side and a flat corner on the other. I got an office call at home and put the gift wrapping down for about a half hour and didn't pay attention when I did the other side."

"I'll talk to her and get her talking again."

"Don't."

"How is the firm? Are you settling in well?" Mill asked as they made a right and started walking down Main Street.

"We just got a big contract for a movie studio to redo their logo and all of their branding materials."

They talked for a few more blocks on Main Street when Ellie came to a sudden stop and looked over her shoulder across the street.

"What is it?" Mill asked.

Ellie slightly shook her head to refocus on what she thought she just saw.

"What?!" Mill asked again.

"James Winnington III."

"What about him? I'm all for you getting back in the relationship game after Stephen, but dear, for heaven's sake, please not *him*."

"No, not that. He's having an early supper over at the Greek diner across the street. I saw him in the window seat."

"And why would that make you stop here on Main Street as if you'd heard an artillery shell?"

"Because he was with someone."

"Who?"

"*Ripped Jeans.*"

"Sweetie, are you losing your mind? I know Stephen's out of your life, but don't lose it on me right here on Main Street."

"I don't know his name, but the fourth person on the seaplane out here was a guy in ripped jeans and a t-shirt that said, 'Stop the Slaughter, Ban Baby Oil.'"

Mill chuckled at the cleverness and said, "I didn't see him or notice him. I only saw you and the investment banker. And what is so special about this man *Ripped Jeans*?"

He and James Winnington III are eating. *Together*. At the Greek diner.

"Why is that so special?"

"Because on the way out here, they never once spoke to each other on the plane. As a matter of fact, I don't think they even acknowledged each other's existence. Those two couldn't be more different. They didn't even get off the plane and walk off together."

"Maybe they were both at the diner and saw each other and the banker was gracious to the other person and asked him to sit with him."

Ellie turned away from the diner window so she wouldn't be seen and faced the village bookstore's big display window that had a huge poster and stacks of *Lonesome Dove*. Ellie could see herself and her grandmother in the reflection. At a rather tall five feet, eleven, she was almost a foot taller than her grandmother. Her bobbed blond hair was parted on the side and the window was so clean, she could see some of her early summer freckles. Her periwinkle eyes shown just a little in the glass as well, as did the dark circles under them representing the very little sleep she'd gotten over the past several days.

Turning back around, she asked in the direction of the diner, "Now, why would that be?"

Mill threaded her left arm into Ellie's right arm and said, "C'mon, let's get home and get you some lobster rolls and white wine out on the patio."

Mill had never remarried after her husband's demise at Shinnecock Hills. She had a painting done of him and hung it prominently in the foyer of their large estate not far from Main Street. Actually, it was Mill's grandmother who, getting tired of travelling almost 15 miles to get groceries, sold 20 acres of their farmland so there could be a real Main Street in Sounion. She'd also financed the building of the local library. At the time of her death, she was the largest employer in Sounion and responsible for the largest chunk of revenue.

Mill opened the front door and Ellie walked into the house she'd been visiting all her life. She lived here every summer, even as an infant. She glanced and did her fun little reverential salute to the grandfather who would sneak her doughnuts much to his daughter's chagrin. The house was very large and very open and Ellie could see through huge French doors and behold the magnificent ocean.

"The Town Fair was in the back right there on the beach," Mill pointed to the back portion of her property.

"How was clean-up?"

"Don't ask. That was the one aspect I didn't think entirely through when I volunteered to host on our property, though it was wonderful community time. I've told them I'll do it again next year. All the high school lacrosse teams: Freshman, JV, Varsity Boys, and Varsity Girls were here for their annual dinner a few weeks later."

"Was Mom there? She's still a legend in this town."

"No, but you heard she donated the funds for the lacrosse field?"

Startled, Ellie said, "Say what you will about Mom, she is quite humble—and quite generous."

"She made them call it 'Millicent Field.'"

"That's quite a daughter you have there, Grandma."

Mill made a dismissive gesture and called out, "Sofia, could we have two of your world famous lobster rolls?"

Sofia, who had the roles of chef-maid-errand-runner-chauffeur-caretaker around the estate came in and belted out, "Hey, girl!" to Ellie with a wide smile and gave her a chiropractic hug inadvertently cracking Ellie's mid-vertebrae. Sofia, was a large Greek woman of about sixty whose family had been in Sounion longer than Mill's family. She wore sandals with khaki shorts, a Hawaiian shirt with toucans in an odd confederacy and a cooking apron. Mill trusted her with everything. She had an enormous suite at the opposite end of the hallway from Mill and down the hall from where Ellie's parents stayed when they were here.

"I've already started the rolls," she said. "You girls have a sit outside and I'll bring them around in a little bit, here's a couple of wine glasses and some lovely Long Island white" and she went back inside.

Ellie and Mill went to the patio and sat down at the table. It was unseasonably warm and dry for a Memorial Day weekend on southern Long Island. The wind came in off the ocean and Ellie wished that the wind could carry her self-doubts away. She tried to reassure herself that she'd just been named President of one of the largest design firms in New York City at the age of 33. It didn't help. Getting dumped is getting dumped. Getting dumped unceremoniously, almost offhandedly after five years, seared into the soul. She opened the bottle, poured a third-of-a-glass for Mill and then proceeded to pour a glass so full to the top for herself she had to do that kid thing where they don't use their hands but bend over and take a big slurp so it won't spill when they pick it up.

"So, you want to talk about that?" Mill asked, looking at her granddaughter's glass, in a whisper as if there were an angry mob of Prohibitionists nearby.

Ellie's eyes filled with tears. She didn't allow herself to cry at work the past several days, and for that matter, wouldn't even cry alone in her own apartment. A few loud sobs in the bathroom as she looked in the mirror. She'd kept saying through gritted teeth in her apartment, "I will not let him get the best of me!"

Mill came over and gave her a hug and Ellie laid her head on the much smaller woman's shoulder. Mill said, "So, even before the maître d', huh?" The way Mill said it was so tender, yet infused with just enough humor that it made Ellie laugh for a moment. Snot blew out of her nose and, like any good grandparent, Mill conjured a handkerchief out of thin air and wiped her nose.

"I do blame myself for the break-up," Ellie said.

"That's like blaming the wall for a crash at the Indianapolis 500."

"Lon, the president and founder of the firm as well as my mentor, said he wanted to retire to Tuscany about eighteen months ago and he kept hinting that I would take over."

"Lon is the one who died of a heart attack a couple of days after he named you president, right? He was a very smart man, you'd done most of the heavy design work for that firm for the last few years."

"The Chief Financial Officer kept saying to Lon that he should be named President and I should just keep designing and I would simply get a larger raise or a percentage of the profits."

"Oh, sure. The profits controlled by this CFO guy being president and *his* salary," Mill said sarcastically.

"But Stephen, at the same time, was going for partner at his law firm."

"He was doing one hundred hour work weeks you told me."

"True, I kept rolling over on law books in the middle of the night. He kept saying almost every week, 'We'll get engaged when I make partner. You *have* to help me make partner.'"

"Your father told me you did everything for him. Hosting the dinners at his apartment because his idea of cooking is stovetop oatmeal. Chatting up the partners at cocktail parties. Looking over his work. I heard you twice caught court-submission errors he made on big cases that would've gotten him *fired* let alone make partner. Upgrading his wardrobe from prep school freshman to actual lawyer. You *made* him partner alright. You were putting in all your time for him and not for yourself."

Ellie looked out over the ocean, gave a wan smile and said, "Guilty, your honor."

"And, the other woman. There is another woman? Is it true what your father says?"

"It's true."

"She isn't/wasn't *really* a . . ."

"She was. One of my male designers confirmed it. Come to think of it, one of my female designers confirmed it as well. They both subscribe to the magazine."

"Did you know before about her?"

"I should've. Over the last six months or so, I've really seen very little of Stephen after he made partner. Heck, I thought we'd get engaged the weekend after he made partner. But as the weeks and months would go by, it kind of blended into dull tableau. I'd phone him and tell him I'm making dinner for the two of us and twenty minutes before he was supposed to be home, he'd call and say, 'Oh, sweetie. I have to work late tonight, you know, the other partners need me on something. I'll be home after midnight.' Twice he didn't come home until dawn. But there was this singular odd aspect to it I never picked up on and, you know, I sort of pride myself on picking up on the little details of life. Little nuances of facts and occurrences. It's really helped my career as a designer, clients really like that about me."

"What was the singular odd aspect you overlooked?"

"He always called from a *pay phone*. Not from his office. I could hear cars going by and people in the background. If he were working late, he'd be calling from his desk underneath a mountain of paper. I would be so hurt that he wasn't coming home, I'm sure I even heard the cars on the street, but it never registered. He couldn't call from the office because he couldn't risk his secretary, or a paralegal, or another lawyer ratting him out to me. It hit me at three in the morning a couple of nights ago."

"*Playboy?* You've got to be kidding."

"The other woman is famous. Seriously. She's been featured in the *New York Daily News* and on *Entertainment Tonight*. When she was an undergraduate at Harvard, she posed for *Playboy* to help make money to fund her dream of going to law school. She went to law school, did well, and Stephen's firm hired her as a first-year and she promptly stole my man. She even left Stephen's firm so there would be no conflict of interest." Ellie looked down at the glass, picked it up, and drank the entire glass in several gulps like it was fresh water in Death Valley, then held the glass up into the sun, inspecting it for flaws as if it was a metaphor for inspecting flaws in her own life and relationships.

"Is there any chance? I mean, do you want him back? Have you even spoken to him?"

Ellie's toe drew an imaginary line on the patio and said in monotone, "They were married at City Hall, nine o'clock this morning. They then went to JFK and took the Concorde to Paris for their honeymoon."

Mill gasped, *"Ye gods and little fishes!"* Which for Mill was like using the f-word as a noun, verb, and adjective all rolled into one. The last time Ellie heard Mill say that phrase was when, as a fourteen-year-old, Ellie had painted a perfectly-rendered enormous Adidas logo on the back of the Mill's garage because, as Ellie pointed to it and said with boundless pride. "I'm really interested in logo design, Grandma! Look!"

Ellie took a deep breath, "And, so. I found out at lunch today, walked down to the Ladies room, threw a Category 5 tantrum—I may have torn a sink off the wall—went back into my office, called for a seaplane reservation at the last possible moment, and the seaplane dropped me into the safest place on the planet I know. Sounion Cove."

Mill put an arm around her, "You know, you're beautiful . . ."

Ellie cut her off, "I'm too tall for most men, Grandma."

Undaunted, Mill said, "You're smart."

"Didn't go to a fancy Ivy League school or law school . . ."

"You're the Presi . . ."

"Grandma. Let me be miserable, please? Tell me some gossip or something. Change the subject."

Sofia came out with the lobster rolls and some homemade potato chips with gorgonzola cheese on them and started walking back to the big house. Mill asked impishly and obnoxiously loudly, "Hey, Sof, do we got any *Playboys* laying around the house? I gotta look up somebody." She was trying not to smile, trying to make it seem like it was an important research task that had to be completed.

Without hesitation, Sofia yelled back equally loud, "Every issue since 1958 somewhere. I love the interviews!" You could tell that Mill and Sofia had been employer and employee for quite a while.

Ellie giggled and at that moment, she got the impression that she just might end up okay.

Chapter 3.

The policeman

"I've made up your bedroom above the garage," Sofia said as she turned to go back in the house.
"Thanks, you didn't have to do that."
"Oh, I was sneaking around in there, looking through drawers and stuff," she smiled.
"Very funny."
"Did you hear about our latest gossip?"
"I'll take anything to get my mind off the past few days," Ellie murmured.
Sofia nodded over to Mill to tell. Mill clapped the palms of her hands down on her thighs and said, "Well, first, we have a new mute cop in town; and second, a real estate firm is trying to build a large hotel at the other end of Main Street. A very large, very expensive hotel."
"A mute cop?"
Mill shrugged, "Not *exactly* mute. It's just he speaks very little. If at all. Maybe I should nickname him 'Calvin' after Calvin Coolidge, who, after being accosted by a woman who bet that she could make him say more than three words, responded, 'You lose.' Our newest policeman is cut from the same cloth. And, he's a former hockey player. He played for the Islanders for a couple of seasons."
"Do I even want to hear about the hotel?" Ellie asked.
"No, you don't."
"Tell me, I feel like I'm immune to bad news for the next half decade."
"A group of 'investors' from Manhattan got in their hunter green Range Rovers and drove out here. They want to build a fifty room—"
"Fifty rooms!" barked Ellie.
"Oh, it doesn't stop there, they want to open high-end boutiques all down Main Street so the glitterati can walk along and buy stuff."
Ellie made a *time out* symbol with her hands. "Time out, time out. Where is this hotel going? On this side of Main

Street is all houses and the cove and they can't just tear down houses and build a hotel." She pointed in the opposite direction from where they were, "On the other side of town is a large beach egress and the high school."

Mill nodded her head. "You know the athletic field across the street from the high school?"

"Of course, I do. I played pee-wee lacrosse there starting at age 5."

"They want to make a sizable contribution to the high school athletic fund, and by that I mean a *really* sizable contribution to the athletic fund and move all the athletic fields down Long Pond Road. They are willing to build everything state-of-the-art with new scoreboards, drainage and practice fields."

"Long Pond Road is the mosquito capital of the universe!"

Mill held up a finger, "They brought in an eradication specialist—I guess the correct term is *entomologist*—to the very first meeting as soon as someone mentioned it from the town, and they let the eradication specialist speak for fifteen minutes on how they'd get rid of all of them. They actually went in and eradicated *all* the mosquitoes from this town as a show of good faith. And it certainly worked. Something with carbon dioxide got rid of them. They went from zero percent of the town wanting a hotel to about fifty percent. Overnight."

"I'm guessing no one has told Mother about this? She's the one that contributed all the money to have the lacrosse field rebuilt."

Mill shook her head like she'd heard a faux pas during a State Dinner at the White House. "No, and no one is going to tell her just yet."

"It won't be me."

"Does she know about the breakup?"

"I'm guessing Dad told her."

"A little cold not reaching out to your own daughter."

Ellie got sad again, "I did call her phone a few times when I was bottoming out. Got the message machine and no return call."

The two of them talked for a few more hours and finally Mill said she wanted to get some sleep. Ellie retreated to her bedroom which was above the three-car garage.

Fearing a restless night, Ellie busied herself with work: A big client pitch in the city week after next, revisions on a logo for a new cable channel that was to be launched around Labor Day, and accounting spread sheets. It was three when she finally fell over wearing the same clothes she had on when she flew out.

By some miracle that would've confounded any Polysomnography, Ellie slept straight through—save for a short dream that featured Stephen—until eight the next morning when she heard shuffling amongst the white pulverized clamshells that made up her grandmother's driveway.

She got out of bed feeling like her head weighed as much as an Easter Island statue, looked out the window and observed a policeman, about her age, shuffling around the driveway, looking out into the ocean. Opening the curtains to an already opened window, she called down, "Can I help you?"

He turned, smiled, and said, "Yes."

Ellie gave him a fair amount of time to elaborate, gave up, and said, "You'll have to give me a little more than that."

He made a *quiet down* gesture with his hands, and said, "I don't want to wake anyone up."

"You're without success."

He looked out at the ocean, and back up to her, nodded, and moved closer to the window, speaking softly, "Didn't want to knock on the front door until eight. Early."

"My grandmother is usually up at five. It's likely she's in her garden out back or reading in her library. Hold on."

Ellie looked in the mirror, she knew she was prettier than most, if they didn't care about the height thing, but her reflection looked like a drawing from an elementary student— an elementary student that didn't like her. She shook out her hair a moment, pinched the apple of her cheeks a few times so she wouldn't look like a cadaver, opened the door, and walked down the stairs onto the driveway.

The policeman was taller than her by about four inches, was extremely well built, this was accented by his short-sleeved uniform shirt that was doing a lousy job containing his large biceps. He had hazel eyes and a five o'clock shadow, though it was eight in the morning.

"How can I help you officer?"

"A body washed up on shore last night."

"That's terrible! What time?"

"Late. Coroner said that T.O.D. was about eleven."

"T.O.D.?"

"Time of Death."

"And?"

"You may know him."

"Me?"

"Someone saw you getting off the seaplane with him yesterday."

"Did he have on ripped jeans? Or a suit?"

"How did you know that?"

"Know what?"

"That he had ripped jeans."

"One of the passengers had on ripped jeans, the other had on a three-piece suit."

"Did you talk to him on the plane?"

"Not really, he only mentioned if the plane crashed, I would die before him because I was in the front seat next to the pilot. Oh, I asked him what he did for a living and he, and I'm quoting exactly, said, 'Absolutely nothing.'"

"Not necessarily," he said.

"'Not necessarily' what?"

"You wouldn't die before him in a plane crash." He continued, "No name?"

"No. He drowned?"

"Looks like he went out for a swim and came back dead, but something isn't right."

"Like what?"

"He had mild onset hypothermia, you know how cold the ocean water is, even in late May. Coroner took blood out of him to see if he was drunk. Actually, what it looks like, if you can believe it: He *swam* himself to death."

"Doesn't that happen fairly often out here? Maybe he got disoriented and swam further out or took a bad angle against a rip tide trying to get back in."

"Older folks have heart attacks in the water this time of the year because the heart goes into a fight or flight response with the cold water. This guy swam himself to death. And two other things: Coroner said his right-hip was dislocated like a whale or swatted him, so he only could use his arms and kind of one leg to swim. Can only imagine how much pain he was in, and . . ." He paused.

"And what?"

"Each of his four pockets had cellophane-wrapped large packets of cocaine. I don't know the street value, but it was a lot."

Ellie looked out at the ocean and got a little chill. "He was reading *The Mammoth Hunters* and he wasn't terribly friendly."

"Did he talk to anyone else on the plane?"

"No, but . . ."

"But what?"

"Excuse me," Ellie stuck out her hand. "This is my grandmother's house, I'm—"

Mill came out of the house and said, "Hi, Claude."

"Morning, Mill," he said with a wave and a smile.

"Trouble?"

"Yep, sorry. Body washed up last night. This—" he nodded over to Ellie.

"Officer Claude Morgan, newly-minted policeman of Sounion Cove, this is my granddaughter, the fair Ellie Pincrest of Manhattan."

Claude shook her hand, did not check her out—the way most men did when they met her as he was clearly lost in thought—and said, "Mill, sorry to come out so early. I've been up all night with this. My captain is wanting answers."

As if on cue, his walkie-talkie squawked and he grabbed it like he was at the O.K. Corral. "Yes, Cap. Here now. Talking to her. Back shortly."

Mill whispered to Ellie, "As you can see, we're trying to get him to augment his lexicon."

He turned back to Ellie and said, "You were just saying something else about the deceased?"

"It's just that, the person with the ripped jeans didn't speak to anyone on the plane, save for me and that was very briefly. But, when my grandmother and I were walking down Main Street to go home, he was in the diner eating with the person who was sitting next to him on the seaplane."

"They didn't speak at all on the plane?"

"I don't think they even *looked* at each other on the plane. As a matter-of-fact, the two of them got off the plane separately and walked separately onto Main Street because the other guy was talking to my grandmother and I."

"What's his name?"

Mill said it with a flair and a roll of her hand, "James Winnington III." Mill ran into the house, came back, and handed Winnington's business card to Claude.

He turned it over several times in his hand. "It's Saturday. No one will be at his office phone. Maybe I can track him some other way. Did he say where he was staying?"

"No," Ellie said shaking her head.

Officer Claude Morgan got back into his patrol car and made his way back to the police station.

Chapter 4.

Confrontation on Main Street

Over breakfast, Ellie and Mill talked about *Ripped Jeans*. It gave Ellie the creeps to know that she'd spoken, if ever so briefly, with a person now dead.

"Come on, let's walk into town, I've got to pick up a new American flag. Those March storms made it look like it was flying over Fort McHenry," Mill said.

They met up in the driveway and headed out to Main Street. In front of the hardware store was a feisty forty-something mom handing out flyers bellowing, "NEW HOTEL EMERGENCY TOWN MEETING AT ONE TODAY AT THE HIGH SCHOOL GYM!"

Ellie took one. The paper was chartreuse and Xeroxed on it from an original hastily written in magic marker, "GREEDY REAL ESTATE TYCOONS ARE TRYING TO TAKE OVER OUR TOWN. STOP THEM. 1 P.M. TODAY."

"What's that?" said a foppish James Winnington III appearing out of nowhere. He had on madras shorts, a pink Oxford button down, and standard penny loafers with subway tokens instead of pennies.

Ellie noticed the subway tokens and made mention of them. He said, "Sometimes, after a big deal has gone down successfully, I'll get so hammered, I know that I can always get home, even if I've lost my wallet because the tokens are in my shoes."

Mill said, "I don't know if I should find that clever or deeply sociopathic."

James Winnington III gave her a little squeeze on the arm and a wink. "Little bit of both, Grams."

"How did you get clothes? You didn't even have a bag yesterday. Do you have a place out here? Are you staying out here?" asked Ellie.

He changed the subject, reached over, and took the flyer from Ellie's hand. "Tycoons?" he said mockingly as he made eye contact with the flyer shouter. He spoke loudly so others could hear as he held the flyer aloft. "Please come and hear exactly the benefits to this community! I shall be speaking myself along with other tycooooooooooons!"

The flyer shouter considered first punching him in the face, then fantasized about getting in her car and running him over, but chose walking down a block and resuming her handing out. James Winnington III blew a kiss to her back, batted his eyelashes, and put his hands over his heart like a love-sick silent movie star.

"Did you hear?" Ellie asked.

"Hear what?" he replied.

"The other guy—the other passenger—in the plane besides you. He's dead."

"You're kidding. We were just with him."

"Drowned."

"Dude was barely here and goes off gets himself drowned? Was he drunk?"

"Police don't know. They mentioned it was like he swam himself to death, and he had a dislocated hip."

"Huh. Crazy," but he sounded disinterested. "I didn't know him."

"What are you talking about? I saw you with him."

"With who?"

"With *whom*," Mill said.

"The guy with the ripped jeans. The guy who sat next to you on the plane," Ellie said.

"Just because I was sitting next to him on a seaplane doesn't mean I knew him or had dinner with him after." He began to walk away.

Ellie grabbed his arm and said, "I *saw* you eating with him at the Greek diner."

Winnington looked at Ellie's hand clutching his arm for a moment and then turned his gaze to her eyes, "Look, I never talked to him in my life. I don't even think we said hello to each other."

"Don't try to gaslight me!" Ellie said a little too loud. A passerby turned to look at her and stopped.

He shrugged his shoulders with a smile, "Sorry, wasn't me."

She poked a finger into his chest, "I'm not asking you to boil the ocean, just admit you were eating dinner with him."

Winnington gave her a condescending shake of the head.

Ellie turned to her grandmother, "You saw them together, right?"

"I'm sorry, there was too much glare from the setting Sun yesterday, I couldn't see in the diner as well as you. I only remember the conversation on the dock right after you landed."

Ellie turned back to him and said, "Stop it. You were there."

He shrugged again, "Sorry, if you say so, but I wasn't. Does it help that I did eat at the Greek diner yesterday? Will that help you?"

"Don't patronize me!" Again, too loud. Another two people stopped to watch.

"Look, I think you're causing a scene," he said calmly putting his hand on her shoulder.

She knocked it away, "Don't touch me! You were with him!" And she marched off with Mill in tow. They went up three blocks to the Greek diner. Theo, the owner since Zeus was in high school, was working the register.

He saw Mill and Ellie and grabbed two menus and spoke in a thick Greek accent. "Mrs. Mill, zo glahd."

Mill nodded and said, "Theo, oh sorry, not eating today. We just have a quick question."

He smiled, took Mill's hand and said, "If you are propozing, I accept!"

Mill smiled and said, "Oh, thank you, Theo, maybe not today. My granddaughter has a question for you."

"Oh, zhe is much too young for me! I cannot marry one zo young! It is forbidden! I have known this young lady since zhe is up to my knee." he said with mock incredulity. He was enjoying his little comedy routine that he did for most of the older women in the village.

Ellie asked, "Did you see two men eating together here at dinnertime? One had a three-piece suit on, the other had ripped jeans."

"*Nai, nai.* Yes, yes. They were here."

Ellie said, "Ha! I *knew* it!"

"But—" Theo interjected. "They did not eat *together*. The suit, fancy-fancy, he simply asked if he could use the bathroom and I said okay, as long as he eats here sometime over the weekend."

Ellie's heart sank. "I saw them *together*," she implored.

"He did not eat here. The other did. Of course, I could be wrong. You know how it is here at dinner time—run, run, run—for me. Maybe they did eat together. Who knows?"

"Thank you," Ellie said as they left. She didn't mean it.

Chapter 5.

Trapped in the bathroom

The Town Meeting at the gym gave off its own electricity even as Ellie and Mill walked up to the door. They were twenty minutes early and the place was already packed. There was no air conditioning, because there aren't air conditioners in high schools less than a half mile from the ocean, but they sure needed it today. If for nothing else, to cool down the hot heads who were already trying to stir up defiant chants.

Near the tip-off circle at half court was a dais of four chairs: Mayor Archie Richardson, who was entering the last six months of a fifth term. He'd already announced he was retiring as he was in his mid-sixties. Next to him was a man in half-glasses with the words *Don't mess with me, I'm a very good attorney and I will eat you* written all over him. James Winnington III was in the third spot still wearing the same clothes from his dust-up with Ellie. He was looking immensely pleased with himself, and in the fourth chair, was a good-looking man of about fifty, in a smart blue blazer, khakis, crisp white shirt, no socks, and the same standard penny loafers as James Winnington III. He gave off the impression that he could see you, but you couldn't see him.

Two minutes before the start, the crowd was getting raucous, it seemed like everyone in the village was here. Ellie even saw Mac the Pilot. A group of about twelve moms started a chant, "Hell, no! Hotel's gotta go!" After seven or eight rounds of this, practically the entire gymnasium was chanting it. The guy in the blue blazer just smiled like a movie star on a red carpet. When people around Mill noticed *she* wasn't chanting it, they stopped, then others saw them, and the chant petered out.

Archie Richardson banged his gavel and spoke into the microphone. He had a little name placard in front of him that read, "Mayor Richardson." He wore cargo shorts and a white Lacoste shirt that might've predated the old crocodile, René Lacoste, himself. He was the pediatrician in town and this was probably the first time he'd seen this much anger directed at him. He knew pretty much everyone in the gym and had known a couple generations of moms especially.

"Please," he said simply trying to get some order. Ellie had known Archie Richardson for a long time. Truth be told, the first boy she ever made out with was Archie's nephew at a town summer camp when she was thirteen.

When it quieted down, he said, "Thank you. I'd like to have this be an efficient meeting and it will last about an hour. There is a proposal in front of both the planning commission and the town board for a hotel to be built across from the high school."

Several boos and raspberries were uttered along with cheers and whistles and he tapped his gavel like a tweed-clad Scotsman cleaning his pipe. "Excuse me, excuse me, please. This is Memorial Day weekend and we should all be out with our families, but I thought this was important enough to bring together the community and the firm proposing the hotel. I'd like to introduce, to my left, Morris Barkwell, attorney for the firm; and to his left, James Winnington, an investment banker who is doing the financing for the project; and, to my far left, Roger Michter, President of Michter Properties to make a brief presentation.

The good-looking man of about fifty at the end of the dais, got up and went to one of the two standing microphones that were to be used for comments from the community and said, "Hello, welcome, and thank you for giving me the opportunity to speak about something we think is very exciting. Simply put, we plan to create a hotel with architecture that will match the look and feel of this marvelous village called Sounion Cove, with fifty rooms, a world-class restaurant, and a day spa for those who aren't staying over. It will bring several hundred high-paying construction jobs to Long Island in the short-term, and countless jobs in the long-term. Our impact studies show that it will be small enough not to overwhelm the downtown area, but large enough and nice enough to make sure shops and businesses in Sounion will thrive for decades. Thank you." And he sat down with the self-satisfaction of a boxer who'd just made Muhammad Ali take a standing eight count.

About six dozen hands shot up. Archie said, "Okay, okay. Comments and questions please. I am going to keep each question and answer to three minutes. We are going to set the basketball clock to three minutes for each person."

First, was a college-aged girl with a Hunter College sweatshirt and way too much eyeliner and black hair dye holding a sign that said, "The scariest thing in my life should be grades!" In a tiny voice that matched neither the cleverness nor the ferocity of her sign said, "You have to *leave* here. You are not *wanted* here. You are not *needed* here."

Second, was an older mom who shouted so loudly into the mic there was high-pitched feedback so everyone put their fingers in their ears. No one remembered what she said.

Third, fourth, and fifth were questions about rezoning laws and construction vehicles and safety of the kids.

Several pro-hotel folks used their three minutes to talk about jobs and Sounion and Long Island shouldn't be left behind.

Frankly, it all got a little boring very quickly because the lawyer with the half-glasses hijacked everyone's three minutes with legal doubletalk when he answered their questions. Ellie's mind began to wander. She thought of *Ripped Jeans*, then she glanced at James Winnington III. It rankled that he had lied to her.

She looked over at a person who had on a hat with the logo of a large baseball equipment manufacturer. Ellie had designed the logo a few years ago. He was in his mid-twenties, dressed a little down and maybe out of place for Sounion with denim shorts and a flannel shirt. He was sitting in her row about eight feet from her on her left, and though he was looking at the dais, the logo on the hat was pointed directly at her because he had it on askew ninety degrees to the right. She was smiling to herself when all of a sudden he nodded, like he was acknowledging something. He then made a subtle finger-pointing gesture to the door and got up and started walking down the bleachers and toward the exit. Ellie noticed the person he was motioning to was James Winnington III.

About four seconds later, Winnington, who hadn't spoken yet during this soiree got up and shuffle jogged in the subtle, but manly gesture of *I've got to go to the Men's room, I'll be right back* and headed for the exit.

Ellie, motivated by the lie and the standoffishness on Main Street that morning, followed *Skewed Hat* out the door. She lingered near the exit for about thirty seconds to ensure her stealth and went out the door and into the large anteroom where the ticketing and concessions were sold during basketball season.

Her stealth was immediately negated because in that large room, there were only three people: James Winnington III, *Skewed Hat,* and her.

The two men were talking to each other and hadn't seen her yet. *Skewed Hat* was saying something to Winnington and they both nodded their heads. Ellie was standing at the door and the banker looked over *Skewed Hat's* shoulder and saw her; a frown forming on his face.

She acted like she was walking down the hall to the Ladies room, went in through the two doors and over into a stall and closed it.

Twenty seconds later, someone came in, and she swore she heard the bolt slide over to lock the bathroom entrance door. There was silence as the second person didn't go into a stall.

Ellie opened the stall door and right in front of the stall was James Winnington III.

"Hi," he said. He was smiling, but not with his eyes.

"You've got some cheek. Get out of here!" Ellie yelled.

He acted like he didn't hear her. "Tell me, are you following me or something?"

"Are you joking? I'm in the Ladies Room, and, if you haven't noticed, so are *you*."

"Why don't you like me?" he asked.

"I don't know you, but you're off to the worst start in history and you're trending downward."

"Why did you say I was with that other guy in the Greek diner when you know I wasn't?"

"Because I saw you in there with him. And it wasn't a case of mistaken identity, there's no one in Sounion on the Friday of Memorial Day weekend in a three-piece suit on Main Street."

"I wasn't with him," he gave her a reptilian smile.

"Knock it off, I'm not an imbecile."

"Did you tell the police I knew him?"

"A policeman came to my house this morning because they knew we were all on the plane. Yes, I told the policeman I saw you with him at the Greek diner. That's it."

He moved closer to her and stroked her shoulder. "Now, kitten. Why don't I believe you?"

Ellie was getting more angry than frightened. It also helped she was about the same height as him. She knocked away his hand from her shoulder and said, "Look, I don't care what you believe. If you're doing your stupid coke lines with that guy, that's none of my business. Actually, I should probably make it my business."

He acted like a wounded puppy and said through a frowning face, "And you're the person gonna help me?"

"Just leave me alone."

"I don't touch the stuff—just for the record. If you've just accused me of doing coke to the police, I'll have both my personal lawyer and corporate lawyer sue you and keep suing you! You'll never work in Manhattan again."

"I only said you were with him. I don't care about anything you do."

She moved around him and he grabbed her arm like he was contemplating tearing it off, but in a quiet voice, he said, "You know, I'm not the kind of person to trifle with."

"Neither am I," and in one quick motion, she kneed him in the crotch. He tried to hold on, but the nausea in him rose faster than a boiling pot of pasta. He tried to follow her on all fours and grab at her ankles, but Ellie beat him to the door, and with adrenaline-rushed shaking hands, unbolted and flung open the door only to meet Sounion policeman Claude Morgan.

Next to him was a woman with four-year-old daughter. "Finally!" the mother yelled as she pushed past the policeman.

"Mom! There's a man on the floor of the bathroom!"

The Mom turned, glared at Ellie and said, "Really? You couldn't wait until you got home for your little romantic interlude?"

"What?! I . . . that's not what . . ." Ellie was too flummoxed to say anything.

"I can't go to the bathroom with a man in here!" cried the girl.

"Out!" yelled the mom at the slowly recovering Winnington.

Officer Morgan walked over and helped up James Winnington III who at that moment must of wondered if there were going to be any more roman numerals climbing around his family tree. Morgan was taller than the slowly unfolding banker. When he finally stood straight, Morgan looked down upon him and proclaimed, "James Winnington III, I presume? *Mon Dieu*. Isn't this my lucky day. I've been looking all over for you. Why don't we go out into the hallway and chat a moment, shall we?"

Chapter 6.

The roundhouse

"We were having a little romance, officer. We had met on the plane yesterday and then got together last night. I just wanted to keep the ball rolling if you know what I mean," JWIII said.

"Are you out of your mind?!" Ellie yelled. "He went in there to intimidate me."

Officer Morgan said to Winnington, "It sure seemed to me like me you were in a little distress on the floor, there Mr. Winnington,"

"She's a tiger when we're—you know—doing it," JWIII said with self-satisfaction.

Ellie's anger, hurt and shame over the past week intersected at that moment and she impulsively took a roundhouse swing at JWIII. He ducked and Ellie' connected with Claude Morgan square in the jaw at the exact moment the mom and the little girl came out of the Ladies room. "Mom!" the little girl exclaimed, "She's hitting the nice policeman! She's hitting the nice policeman!" She ran over to Ellie and started punching Ellie's long legs with her tiny fists.

Completely flabbergasted by the last few minutes: threatened, falsely-accused, hitting a police officer, and now being a very poor example to the youth of America, Ellie passively looked down at the girl hitting her until her mother told her to stop. The mother and daughter each gave another glare at Ellie and she could only imagine the gossip that would be around the village by supper tonight. For Pete's sake, everyone in town was in the gym. *Mill's granddaughter—yes, the tall girl who's the big shot in Manhattan—she slugged Claude Morgan today after being caught having sex with a man who wasn't her serious boyfriend in the ladies room of the high school! Oh, Mill must be devastated! Wonder if the boyfriend will dump her now that she's cheating on him so brazenly!*

Officer Morgan smiled while opening and closing his jaw, "Thanks, I needed that," mimicking the classic commercial.

Meanwhile, JWIII was elated and wasn't trying to hide it.

"I'm-I'm sorry!" Ellie said remorsefully. She hoped the ground could swallow her whole.

The smile on Morgan's face transformed into a steely focus on JWIII. "You know what I saw? All kidding aside there, Mr. Winnington, is a young woman with all of her clothes on trying frantically to get out of a Ladies room and a man on the floor with a purple face because he'd been kicked where he'd prefer not to be kicked."

"Oh, you've got it all wrong," JWIII then whispered, "Truth is, we started going at it, she thought better of it and started to run out. I simply tripped over my pants."

Morgan gave him a cold look and whispered back, "Mr. Winnington, I was born at night, but I was not born last night. What I'm really interested in was your conversation with the *other* passenger on the seaplane, the guy with the ripped jeans."

"What conversation?"

"You were with him at the diner."

"That's a lie! Talk to the owner of the diner!"

"That I will most certainly do, I'm just giving you the opportunity to tell me the truth."

"I am telling you the truth. I was at the diner, but was not with the guy with ripped jeans."

"The owner may not have seen you together, he may have been doing other things."

"I've got nothing to hide. If you keep harassing me, I'll be going to your superiors! We're trying to do good things in this town and you're trying to use police intimidation to stop us. You know what? That sounds like a very good idea, that lawyer you saw in the gym there today will be contacting your superiors first thing Tuesday morning. You may be out of a job very soon, Officer!"

JWIII smugly walked back into the gym.

"What was that all about?" Morgan asked Ellie.

"I saw him with the *Ripped Jeans* guy yesterday at the diner, then the *Ripped Jeans* guy ends up dead not far from Mill's house. Then I noticed a guy with a skewed hat motioning to him to talk outside the gym. I followed thinking they wouldn't see me, but there was no one in the anteroom so they saw me. I made it seem like I was going to the bathroom. He followed me in and wanted to know if I'm following him."

"Are you following him?"

"I just wanted to know what he was doing."

"Why?"

"Because he lied to me about seeing the guy that got murdered."

"You're going to be an investigator now?"

Ellie looked out the big glass doors, "I just don't like being lied to."

"Did someone else lie to you?"

Ellie walked away without saying goodbye.

Chapter 7.

A surprise visitor

Mill and Ellie walked back to Mill's house after the gym meeting. The police-slugging / sex-on-the-bathroom-floor gossip was coming her way and she was just going to have to deal with it. She knew pretty much everyone in the village and Mill was likely the most respected person in town, so she tried to tamp down her anxiety.

They made stops at the grocery store for vegetables and the fish market for some swordfish to grill tonight. When they got home, a hunter green Range Rover was in the driveway and next to it was Roger Michter.

He waved and said, "Howdy, howdy! So glad to see you!"

Mill looked at Ellie and said, "What the what?"

He walked up to both of them and shook their hands, "Roger Michter, Michter Properties. Oh, let me take those grocery bags from you. You know, I put myself through college working in a grocery store."

"What are you doing here, Mr. Michter?" Mill said.

Michter was a couple of inches taller the Ellie, had the athletic build as was becoming *en vogue* for men who were overachievers in the business world. He had blue eyes, flawless teeth, salt and pepper hair, and a deep tan. He still had on the khakis, blue blazer, oxford shirt, and sockless shoes he had on at the gym. Smiling brightly and taking a deep breath, he said, "Well, I'm here to ask your granddaughter to do some work for us. Her reputation proceeds her. I read the article about her in the *New York Times*. Wow, named President of one of the top logo design firms in New York City at the age of thirty-three. A woman! Wow!"

Mill and Ellie let the "A woman!" reference slide.

"What kind of work?" Ellie asked.

"A logo, of course," he said. "A logo for my hotel. I'm going straight to the top to ask that you handle our logo and branding. It's quite a peach of an assignment if you think about it. We're not some fly-by-night firm."

Ellie's instinct for both growing business and simultaneously being creative kicked in. It ran up against a wave of distrust of this hotel. She didn't dislike Michter personally, he actually seemed nice. He was in business and she did logos for people who were in business. People at her firm were dependent on her to get more work into the studio. Since the article in the *Times*, the firm got a lot of work in exactly this way.

"You know, we're quite expensive," she said.

"Absolutely, absolutely. Don't I know? If you want to be the best, you've got to hire and nurture the best. And that comes at a price. I read what your firm's fees are in the *Times*."

He started a monologue about how much he loved Sounion, how great the hotel was going to be, and just as Ellie's mind started to wander, Michter said, "I'll be paying half of your firm's fees up front." He handed her a check right then and there.

Ellie told him what they usually did for logo and branding a hotel and the process. She said they asked a lot of questions up front and she would deliver the questions to wherever he was staying in the village.

"I'm renting a house down on the beach. Beautiful view, beautiful view. Here is my card and I'll write the house phone number and address."

"I do have one stipulation for the project or I won't do it."

Momentarily puzzled, Michter asked, "What is it?"

"James Winnington III."

"What about him? Do you want me to fix you up with him? Would you two be a good match?"

"Quite the opposite. If he's involved in any way—and I mean, I don't want to even see him or speak to him in passing or have him show up for a meeting—we won't do it."

Michter looked at her for a few moments and gave her a smile of satisfaction, reached out his hand to shake hers, and said, "Done. I will ask that you put this in the highest gear possible for quick completion."

"I may have some more questions after we get started."

"Certainly, certainly." He looked over at the house and then at Mill and said, "What a gorgeous house. What year was it built?"

Mill said, "My grandmother originally built it in 1886, the Hurricane of '38 blew it into the ocean like most of the houses in Sounion, and my mother rebuilt it."

"What. A. Treasure," he said admiringly, shook both their hands, hopped into the Ranger Rover and drove off.

"You must be good at your job," Mill said. "You go away on a three-day vacation and you still get big projects."

Ellie smiled and said, "I suppose I should go up to my room and get that contract together and the questions I'd like answers to before we start designing."

"Quite a flatterer he was, leading with the *Times* story."

"Funny thing about that *Times* story: I was having the worst hair day ever because I'd worked until two the night before and when I walked into the office at eight having sort of showered and gotten ready for work because we were on deadline, the *Times* photographer had all the lights set up for the shoot. I ended up looking like a cross between a driver's license photo and a bad Polaroid. And two wrongs definitely do not make a right when it comes to photography."

Mill gave her a hug and said, "You're the most beautiful thing I've ever seen. Let me know when you're ready and we'll drive over to Michter's."

Chapter 7.

The bedroom above the garage

Ellie walked up the stairs to her bedroom above the garage.
It had been her room in Sounion since she was fifteen. Mill had it built and ran water and electricity to it about the time Ellie became a teenager because she understood her daughter *and* her granddaughter. Her daughter was tough and insensitive. She understood her daughter had to be like that as an E.R. doctor or she'd hurl herself off the hospital roof. In the first hour of every night of her work (and most E.R. work is done at night), Dr. Pincrest saw more horrific things than most people saw in a lifetime. She ran the department, replacing a male doctor who'd had a nervous breakdown at fifty and now painted water colors in Idaho. She had a reputation with nurses and techs to push them to the limit, because she went to the limit. She saved lives and second place meant death. She was loud, standoffish, and had a husband who wasn't around to take it out on when needed.

On the other side, she had Ellie. Tough, defiant, very likely more intelligent than her mother and with a sharper tongue—Ellie could quote Spinoza in an argument one moment and turn around and swear at her mother like a longshoreman—yet never, ever swore at her father. But, Ellie Pincrest had a marked flaw: she was extremely sensitive. Her mother's constant criticisms weren't so much like a knife; they were like a scimitar. Ellie could stand her ground against her mother anytime, any day, and give it right back with compound interest. But when she went back to her room, she would lie face down on her bed, put one pillow on her face and two pillows over her head and cry hard until she fell asleep.

When Ellie was a freshman in high school with her father away on a concert tour, Dr. Pincrest came home unexpectantly from the hospital at eleven instead of her usual time and found, in her living room on Sutton Place, a shirtless fifteen-year-old boy staring at her like a deer in headlights. Having not heard her mother come through the front door of the apartment, Ellie came out of the kitchen, shirtless, with some chips and soda. She dropped both when she saw her mother.

The fight that ensued was epic. The neighbor across the hall, after listening intently (and gleefully) with his door open, eventually grew tired of the caterwauling, called the police, and they were there in five minutes to hear the crescendo of the fight.

After all was calmed down and the police left, the fight started again over hot cocoa at the kitchen table, Dr. Pincrest said something that can't be repeated here, but it was enough for Ellie to calmly get up from the kitchen table, walk out the front door without a coat on one of the coldest nights of the year, take the subway to Penn Station, and catch the last Long Island Railroad train out to Sounion—a two hour ride. She walked over to Mill's and knocked on the door.

No words were spoken. Ellie was practically asleep on her feet, so Mill simply led her outside, across the driveway to the detached garage and up the newly built stairs to the bedroom suite she'd constructed for her granddaughter above the garage. She opened the door and turned on the lights for her and said, "I was pretty sure this day was coming between you two."

The bedroom was gorgeous with a huge window that looked out onto the ocean. It was two-thirty in the morning. It was the kindest moment of Ellie's life, and she knew it. Mill had decorated the place tastefully. She did put up one poster, that of the logo of the band *Van Halen*. Ellie pointed to it and said with grateful tears filling her eyes, "I don't like *Van Halen*. Do I have to keep that up?"

Mill, putting her arm around Ellie said, "I asked the kid at the poster shop what everyone was listening to in 1986 and he said, '*Like, you know, Van Halen.*' So I took a chance. Take it down in the morning. Get some sleep. I'll call your mother and let you know you're okay. I'm guessing she's called the F.B.I. by now."

That was the first time Ellie knew that Mill could convince her that everything was going to be alright.

Eighteen years later, as Ellie opened the door, the first thing she saw was the faded *Van Halen* poster. As God was her witness, Ellie understood symbolism, heck, she drew symbols everyday as a logo designer, and that poster was the last thing that ever coming down in this bedroom.

Chapter 8.

A party

Ellie spent a couple hours putting together the contract for logo development and all the applications of the logo and two dozen questions to find out his preferences about logos, especially hotel logos. The secret behind Ellie's firm's success was they listened a lot upfront and then developed very precise, simple logos that resonated across a broad spectrum of people.

There was a little intercom in Ellie's room that connected her to several rooms in the big house and she got ahold of Mill and said, "Ready, you want to go?"

"Ready."

Mill went into the garage as Ellie walked down the stairs. They got into Mill's "Irish Green" Karman Ghia with eight gazillion miles on it, but looked like it had only several hundred miles. Ellie couldn't understand how this car survived in all the salt air, but it did.

They drove a few miles down Beach Road to Michter's place. There were several cars there and a Dixieland band somewhere in the background.

Michter's place was gorgeous, it was mostly glass with panoramic views of the water, tasteful, and featured wonderful landscaping and surrounded by sand dunes which gave it an even more private feel. As they walked up the driveway, the door opened and a woman about Ellie's age, slender, fit, with auburn hair and bright blue eyes said, "There you are!" She turned back for a moment and bellowed, "Rah-gerrrr, they'rrrrrrrrrrre here!"

Roger Michter bounded across from another room like a Broadway actor coming on to center stage for final bows after a triumphant performance, "Splendid! Splendid! Come in, come in!"

Ellie noticed that Roger Michter often repeated the same word or phrase. Ellie and Mill went inside the house; it was more gorgeous than the outside. The first thing that caught Ellie's eye was a Picasso hanging over a glass-enclosed fireplace. As she stared at it, the woman with the auburn hair whispered in Ellie's ear, "It's real. Can you believe it? Our renter's insurance here I think is more than the rent. There's a Lichtenstein in the study and several Motherwells throughout the house. Motherwell went to Stanford, as did Roger, so he's especially tickled to see them here."

Ellie offered her hand to the auburn-hair woman, and said, "Hi, I'm—"

Michter swooped in and said, "Jess, this is the person who's going to define us, the famous logo designer Ellie Pincrest. Ellie, this is Jessica Traverts, *caterer extraordinaire.* She puts together the most fabulous parties. And, for a few years now, we've been together in a more romantic way." In addition to Jessica Traverts thick auburn hair and radiant blue eyes, she had a near-perfect creamy complexion to her skin.

"Ahhhh, the 'logo designer to corporate superstars' as it said in the *Times* not too long ago.

Ellie blushed.

"And this is her grandmother, 'Millicent,' or as she's known in town, 'Mill,'" Michter added.

"I hear you pretty much run things out here Mill," said Jessica.

A little speechless, Mill said, "We're just one of the oldest families."

Ellie thought they sure knew a lot about her and her grandmother, but she knew next to nothing about Roger Michter, Jessica Traverts, or James Winnington III for all that mattered.

Roger sidled up to Ellie and said, "James is here, but if you'd like to avoid him, I can give him a high sign to leave you alone. He can be a little much, but aren't all investment bankers?"

"I'll be fine," she said as Jessica put a glass of Rosé in her hand.

Jessica turned and put her arm around Roger Michter and him to her. He gave her a little kiss on the cheek. For an older-younger couple, they were cute.

"Come back to the back and you can see the view, the sunsets at this house are amazing," Michter said.

"How long do you plan to stay in our little village, Mr. Michter?" asked Mill.

"Oh, call me 'Roger!' I'll stay the summer, just to get our ball rolling here in Sounion and get the foundation dug."

Mill asked, "What if they block you?"

Roger said as if he'd been told there'd be no oxygen available for anyone tomorrow, "They won't."

"I know, but just suppose—"

And just then James Winnington III came up through a throng of people and gave Roger a big hug. "This guy! This GUY!" he said pointing at Roger. "This is the guy who has vision. The guy who will get things done in Sounion."

Mill whispered into Ellie's ear, "I've lived in Sounion all my life, and I don't recognize a soul here, do you?"

"No," Ellie whispered back.

"I hear you're doing our logo!" JWIII said.

"Yes, that's why I came, just to drop off the contract and leave some questions." They were in Ellie's hand in an envelope and JWIII snatched it. "I'd like to answer those questions."

In a subtle move, Michter took the envelope out of JWIII's hand and slipped it into his blazer pocket. "These are for me."

He gave Michter a little salute and said, "You're right. My apologies."

"Let's go to the study and I'll sign the contract. Ha! I gave you a check for the work before I signed any contract. What would the dean of my business school say?"

"Golly, we're moving pretty fast," said Ellie.

"No time like right the heck now, am I right?" Michter said as he showed them to the study.

They all entered the study, save for JWIII who practically had the door closed on his nose by Michter. Ellie didn't notice the door closing as she was looking at a large Lichtenstein that was mounted behind a big Herman Miller desk and chair.

Michter stood at the desk and read through the contract, nodded several times and shrugged his shoulders twice. He made a *Mmmmmmm* sound, then took a pen off the desk and signed it above Ellie's signature.

"Thank you," she said. "My firm appreciates the business."

"I'm honored that you would do this project for us. I was worried that we were too small for you."

"I think I'm going to stay out here for the week, I can begin sketching out here immediately."

Michter clinked his glass that was half full of Scotch to Ellie's wine glass and said, "Now who's moving pretty fast? Sketches immediately!" He burst out laughing.

The door opened and Mayor Archie Richardson came in, "Mill, I thought I saw you!"

"Ah, finally someone I know," Mill said.

As Ellie turned and looked back at Mayor Richardson in the doorway, she could see way back in the background in the ultra-modern kitchen, *Skewed Hat*. The hat was off and he was wearing a waiter's jacket, but it was definitely *Skewed Hat*. And again, he was having an animated conversation with JWIII. An animated discussion that neither wanted to be animated.

Ellie was craning her neck to see them and wishing she could read lips when she was interrupted by Michter, "I'll have the answers to your questions in your hands by ten tomorrow morning, that okay with you?"

Snapping around to him, she said, "Great! You want me to pick them up, or do you want to come over to the house?"

"I'll come over to the house, if that's not too much of an imposition."

"No imposition," Mill said.

"Perfect! Let's go back outside and enjoy the sunset."

Ellie was given another glass of Rosé and as Mill chatted over by the fireplace with Mayor Richardson, Ellie went out on the back deck.

"What are you doing here?" It was Mac the Pilot. He stood there a little more cleaned up than usual, but his omnipresent hat was still on. Ellie wondered if it was permanently affixed to his head.

"I'm sort of working."

"That almost sounds sexual."

"You should give the innuendos a little rest, Mac."

"Undoubtedly," he was smoking a cigar and drinking the ultimate May drink—a Mint Julep.

"What are *you* doing here?"

"Oh, I've flown out several of these hotel people. Can you believe it? A fancy hotel in Sounion?"

"Let's see if the town lets them build it."

"Oh, they will. From what I hear, when these hotel people want something done, they'll charm your socks off."

"Like offer a large fee to the granddaughter of the most powerful and popular woman in town to do their logo?"

He took a drag on the cigar, exhaled the smoke and through squinted eyes looking into the setting sun said, "Something like that."

"I'm not sure if it will make a difference."

"Really?" He took another puff on the cigar. "You're here, your grandmother is here, and the mayor is here. Are there any questions?"

"Touché," Ellie said. "So, for a pilot of a four-seater seaplane, you seem to have your pulse on this."

"Do I?" he said through another puff. "I go to these things and listen."

"And what do you hear?"

"The sound of money and jobs coming in. You don't notice it because your view of Sounion and the surrounding area is of my little plane and your grandmother's house, but in reality, a lot of manufacturing jobs have left here and a lot of people are hurting. A lot of middle-class people are hurting, and when that happens, everyone suffers. Cash infusion is king."

Changing the subject, Ellie asked, "Did the police ask you about your passenger? The one with the ripped jeans who was found dead."

"They did."

"And?"

"And, they said he was hit by a whale and swam himself to death. Which I didn't understand in the slightest."

"And what else?"

He shrugged, "They wanted to know how he paid, and I said, with cash. He had a greasy wad in his pocket. He was literally smoothing out bills as he handed them to me. They wanted to know when he made his reservation, and I said, he walked up to the dock a little before you showed up. They wanted to know if you knew him. They wanted to know if Winnington knew him and I said not from what I could tell. The two in the back seats never spoke."

"Seems weird."

"I can't figure out the trauma to his hip. Like a whale tail slapped him. And then he swam himself to death."

"Also said he had cocaine in his pockets."

"That'll slow you down when you're trying to swim for your life," he said flatly.

"Didn't they tell you that?"

"They did. But what am I supposed to do? I didn't know the kid, I don't even know his real name. I don't think the police even know."

"I've been referring to him as *Ripped Jeans* which I guess is insensitive."

"I'm *Mac the Pilot* to you, right?"

"Something like that. Any other words of wisdom?"

Mac the Pilot paused for a long time. At first, Ellie thought he didn't hear. Quietly, he said, "Yeah, watch yourself."

"How's that?"

"I heard you got into a couple of scrapes with him." He nodded over to James Winnington III who was now unabashedly hitting on a comely blond who was wearing an imagination-free dress.

"Scrapes?"

"Watch out for him."

"You don't think I can handle myself?"

"I think that you are the president of a large design firm in Manhattan and you are a woman, which means that most people think you got your job because you are a woman and not from talent and experience. If you mess up even a little, from inside or the outside, you'll be out." He leaned over to the sand next to the outdoor patio and put out his cigar in it. "I'm just a dumb seaplane pilot, but I got eyes."

"You certainly have a lot to say for a guy who claims to be quiet and listens."

He smiled, "Just doing my thing."

He walked away.

Winnington had moved away from hitting on the blonde, to watching Ellie. As soon as Mac the Pilot left, he came over. He stuck out his hand and she recoiled. "Oh, come on, can't we let bygones be bygones."

"Not when they're threatening me in a locked restroom."

And she walked away, but not before *Skewed Hat*, in his waiter's jacket, offered her shrimp cocktail which she promptly declined.

Roger Michter and Jessica Traverts were talking to the lawyer from the dais at the town meeting. Standing next them was Mill showing equal parts sarcasm and disbelief. Ellie had forgotten the lawyer's name until Roger caught her eye and said, "Ellie, would you like to come join us? Our bloodsucking lawyer, Morris Barkwell, is trying to convince your grandmother that all will be well with the hotel. And, frankly, she's not buying it."

Mill bowed a little toward the lawyer; he didn't smile. He looked menacing. He had an athletic build with grayish eyes, grayish hair, and somewhat grayish skin tones. Ellie thought of a logo she once did that was nine shades of black and gray.

"All I'm saying is, we are going to do this by the book and we will have a lot of back-up for our financial projections," said the bloodsucking Morris Barkwell. His attitude on smiling was something akin to *no blue moon, no smile*.

"And all I'm saying," Mill said was, "you can't come into a small seaside village that is usually lagging thirty years behind the rest of the world and say you're going to do something fast, expensive, and everyone will benefit, and not raise a few questions."

"I have answers for all of your questions, Millicent."

Ellie guessed her grandmother had earlier introduced herself to Morris the Bloodsucker as the more formal *Millicent* because she had zero intentions of being friends.

"I'm not sure all of your answers mean much."

"I do have the law on my side, and whether Sounion thinks this is the mid-nineteen fifties is somewhat immaterial. If there is zoning for it, if there is funding for it, it can be built."

"You're building on the ball fields."

Roger Michter piped up, "We will build state-of-the-art ball fields in a nearby place." He waved his arms in the air, "Enough, enough! Let's argue on business time. For now, let's relax, enjoy the sunset, and have a few more drinks."

"Roger," Ellie said, "thank you for inviting us in, but I'd like to get back home and think about some sketches, even before you answer our questions. Do you have a name for the hotel?"

Jessica Traverts cut in, "Of course, we do and it's very simple: *Sounion-by-the-Sea*." Michter gave her a little peck on the top of the head.

Ellie put her arm around Mill and said to Michter, Traverts, and Barkwell, "I like to just play with the letters and see what kind of shapes and lock-ups we can make with an icon and type."

Michter nodded appreciatively, held out his hand and said, "Thanks so much. I'll be by tomorrow with answers to your questions. And don't lose that check before the banks open on Tuesday, it's not an insignificant amount."

As they got back in the Karman Ghia and Mill put the car into first gear, she said, "I don't want to get in your way for a nice project, but if they stray one inch out of their lane on this project, I will land on them like a ton of bricks."

Ellie said, "I think you've made a big impression enough already. They're scared to death of you. Even the lawyer was beginning to throw around legal precedent."

"I just don't want you to get hurt."

"I won't."

Chapter 9.

Drawing

Ellie went to the drafting table in her room. All the other lights were off except for a little light on a flexible arm. She turned on the small Sony radio by the table. *Take My Breath Away* was on.

She liked just sketching letterforms and combinations of letterforms with no other information. These were never chosen as the logo, but always some aspect, some nuance of a letterform always was. She pulled out an oversized sketch pad. Ellie could sketch forty different logos without color off the top of her head without breaking a sweat.

The phone rang in her room. On the third ring, she answered it with her left hand because she had just picked up one of her mechanical pencils with her right.

"Hello," Ellie said a little distractedly.

No one said anything back.

"Mom?" Ellie figured it was her mother who often didn't say hello right away because she was doing something else, but there was usually the hustle and bustle of a hospital going on behind her when she called. There was no background behind the caller.

The silence continued and she thought she heard someone whisper from a distance, "It works," then a slow replacement of the handset.

Ellie caught herself meticulously writing names along a horizontal axis the width of her landscaped-turned sketch pad: *James Winnington III. Ripped Jeans. Skewed Hat. Roger Michter. Jessica Traverts. Morris Barkwell.*

Above each name, she sketched a little icon.

Above *Ripped Jeans*, she drew a tombstone with an "RIP" on it.

Above *James Winnington III*, she drew the vest of a three-piece suit.

Above *Skewed Hat*, she drew the skewed hat he wore at the town meeting.

Above *Roger Michter*, she drew a hotel.

Above *Jessica Traverts*, she drew several hearts with an extending arrow to *Roger Michter*.

Above *Morris Barkwell*, she drew a law book with two bloodsucking fangs going into it.

She added one more because she'd talked to him at the party, *Mac the Pilot*, and drew a seaplane with pontoons and little waves. She put a baseball cap on top of the seaplane because of his omnipresent hat.

She'd been here barely twenty-four hours and she'd met six people she never knew before, plus Mac the Pilot who'd been taking her out to Sounion for a several years now.

She stared at the seven names for a while, making little tweaks to the icons, as if they were to be reviewed by someone in the coming days.

She smiled as she remembered to add an eighth person, a police hat with *Claude Morgan* below it.

Eight.

Her mind, as it often did, started asking questions:

Why did JWIII go out of his way to say he wasn't with Ripped Jeans?

Why did JWIII talk to Skewed Hat? And what were they talking about?

Why did JWIII get so tough after her seeing him talk to Skewed Hat?

Who were those people at that party? If it was a party in Sounion, you would think she—and definitely Mill—would know several people. She could've been at a party eight hundred miles away for as many people as she knew save for Mayor Richardson. Who were they? Investors? Michter certainly needed plenty of backing to get a hotel up in Sounion.

It was Saturday night and she was alone. Her ex-boyfriend used to call Saturday night, "International Date Night" where all over the world, young people were falling in love.

Especially if they fell in love with a first-year lawyer/former Playboy playmate.

She got sad for a little bit thinking they were together in Paris and she was alone here in Sounion with new acquaintances and she wasn't sure if she trusted even one of them—including a policeman. She stopped drawing. She heard Mac's plane go over the house on its way back to Manhattan.

She fell asleep around two with a few too many wet tissues nearby (and a half-empty wine bottle next to her bed) as she wanted to feel sorry for herself. She kept trying to reassure herself that she was successful because of talent and good old-fashioned work ethic. She told herself she was attractive, interesting, and a good conversationalist.

It didn't seem to help.

Chapter 10.

Goon

The next morning, Claude Morgan and his police car were back in Mill's driveway.

Ellie fumbled through putting on shorts, flip-flops, and a RISD sweatshirt and walked down the stairs. She had no idea why she was awake at six in the morning, but for some reason she had heard the car drive up. Her head felt like compressed cotton and her mouth like sandpaper.

He gave a little salute.

"Can I help you Officer Morgan? Isn't it a little early? Is everything okay?"

He didn't know how to say it, so he just said, "No."

"What is it?"

"Another death."

"Who?"

"Some kid. Early twenties. Died of a drug overdose, which, as I understand it, is the first one in the history of this town, and that includes all of the nineteen-sixties and seventies."

"Where did you find him? Do you know who he is?"

"Well, that's why I'm here now. I was just over at the rented house of Roger Michter. He said the kid worked his party last night."

"Did this kid have on a waiter's jacket?"

"No."

"Where did they find him?"

"Couple of Sanitation Department guys saw him sitting there on a park bench and went up to see if he was okay because he was leaning over at an odd angle, but he had his legs crossed. They thought he was okay, just wanted to make sure. When they got close, they saw his shirt was ripped and several hypodermic needle marks were on his arm. As a matter-of-fact, a needle was still in him half full of cocaine."

"Please don't tell me he had a hat on with a logo."

"Hey, how did you know that?"

Ellie sat on the stairs and put her head in her hands. On Friday, she'd talked to someone and now he was dead. She saw a waiter at a party on Saturday, and now he was dead.

"Are you alright?" Morgan put his hand on his shoulder. Ellie restarted the crying from the night before.

"What else do you know?"

"My biggest issue with it was the crossed leg. A drug addict isn't going to demurely sit down, cross his leg, and start shooting cocaine into his arm repeatedly. That doesn't seem anywhere near right."

A shiver ran through Ellie, "No, not right. Anything else pertinent? Don't you call in the F.B.I. or something?"

"No, we don't call in the F.B.I. for someone who's washed ashore and we don't call for a drug overdose. What do *you* know? You were at the party."

Ellie thought for a moment and said, "I've seen him twice: Last night, he was a waiter at the Roger Michter party. I didn't speak to him and didn't see anyone speak to him except for James Winnington. Earlier yesterday—*Has all of this happened over the course of two days?*—I saw him talking to Winnington outside of the gym before I went into the bathroom."

"But you were following this kid, right?"

Ellie didn't really know what to say. Yes, she was following the kid, but she wasn't exactly sure why. "At the town meeting in the gym, he caught my eye, because that hat, a skewed sideways hat—I did the logo for it, so I was noticing it. Then I noticed that he was making some kind of high sign to Winnington. He got up and I followed. I followed because Winnington denied to me earlier in the day that I'd seen him eating at the Greek diner with the other kid who died, the one with the ripped jeans. I thought I was being all stealthy, but I'm an amateur and Winnington saw me talking to him, so I acted like I was going to the bathroom. That's when he came in and locked the door and started haranguing me. Did you talk to Winnington?"

"That cat is hard to find."

"Isn't he staying in Sounion?"

"Well, it appears as if he is in Sounion because he's been seen on Main Street, and at the Town Meeting, and at the Roger Michter party, but no one seems to know exactly where he is staying and no one has a phone number for him out here."

"Do you know the name of the ripped jeans kid or the skewed hat kid?"

"No, neither had I.D. on them."

"So you're kind of nowhere on this?" she asked.

"I've got two dead people who'd never been to Sounion until yesterday."

"I've given you everything I know."

"Somewhere down the line, I hope it's useful."

Ellie hearing the obtuseness of her earlier question, tried to change the subject to talk about anything else. "I hear you played in the N.H.L."

He looked at her a moment, contemplating the change in conversation tactics. She noticed more features about him like the size of his hands, his small waist, but large chest, "Yes, but I wasn't really that good."

"You literally got paid to be a hockey player. That's quite an accomplishment."

"I was an enforcer. Do you know what that is?"

Ellie knew nothing about pro sports, "No, is that some kind of defense player?"

"I've never heard it put that way, but yes. What we really do is keep the order on the ice."

"Wait a minute, don't they have the people in the zebra-striped shirts doing that? The referees?"

"They call penalties and keep time. There are 'enforcers' on each team that make sure that their best players are protected. For example, if our best player takes a cheap shot in the mouth from one of their players, well, it was my job, during the game to send a little message by elbowing him or crashing him into the boards. Or, fighting."

"Fighting! Don't you go to jail for that?! Have you been to jail for fighting?!"

"Whoa, whoa. There is fighting on the ice in hockey. It is used for players to right a wrong, or stand up to another player, or simply to blow off some steam."

"And what happens after the fight? Do you shake hands?"

Claude Morgan unsuccessfully suppressed a laugh, "No, we, uh, just . . . no. We did not shake hands after the fight. But, the crowd would go wild."

"What happens after the fight?"

"You go to the locker room for the rest of the period usually. Sometimes the rest of the game."

"Isn't hockey the sport where you have to sit in the box for a few minutes for a time out or whatever if you are penalized?"

"Yes, it's called the 'Penalty Box,' and some people call it the 'Sin Bin.'"

Now it was Ellie's turn to laugh, like Friday night, snot flew out. Morgan produced a handkerchief. She wiped her nose and asked, "How many years did you play?"

"I played hockey all my life. My mother is French-Canadian and my father was from New York. They divorced when I was very young and I lived with my mother near Quebec City. I grew up speaking more French than English. My father is a large man and I took after him with size and athleticism, so I got into youth hockey as a six-year-old. I was always very good, but I kept growing and growing. Was good enough to play hockey in college, got my degree, and I got drafted."

"Wow, you must've made a lot of money."

He smiled, "No, enforcers are the lowest paid players on the team. They have the smallest skillset."

"You just said you were always good."

"In the N.H.L., everyone is tremendously talented. My father was a cop on the beat in Brooklyn, whenever I visited him down here, he got me boxing lessons. I had just as much aptitude for that, as for hockey. There's no fighting in college hockey so that skillset was never used, but in the first week of my training camp with the New York Islanders—the team out here, the big bruiser for the team tried to teach me a lesson because I was a rookie. He picked a fight with me. He lost. They signed me that day to a contract and kept me on the team. The big bruiser ended up showing me the ropes of the

N.H.L. and became a close friend. Played three years for the Islanders. Best three years of my life. I even have ten goals!"

"Ten goals! Wow! Wait, is that good?"

"For a goon it is."

"You call yourself a 'goon?' You certainly don't look like a goon save for your size."

"Enforcers are often called goons."

"I don't think I like that name: *Goon*."

He chuckled, "I got called a lot things at away games I can't even repeat!"

"And you became a cop after?"

"Yes, it was the thing I wanted to do most after being a professional hockey player."

"Do you have to be an enforcer often as a police officer?"

"Sometimes. It gets messy when they have a gun. Not so messy with a knife, and very definitely not when they just try to straight-up fight me. That usually goes very bad for them. Some guys know who I am and what I used to be, so when they've had a little too much at a bar or during a domestic disturbance, they want to dance when we show up, but they're so drunk they don't even realize how humiliating it is after they're down on the ground."

"Are there a lot of guns here in Sounion?"

"No, but I help out in some other less nice towns when they're down officers because of vacations; we try to rotate around to help out. Just better community work."

"In all the years I've been in Sounion, I've never heard of a murder or a drug overdose."

He began to walk over to his cruiser. "Something's going on and it started Friday. If you see Winnington before I do, let me know. Just don't talk to him. Stay away from him. I probably should tell you to go back into the city, but you seem like a girl who doesn't like to be told what to do."

Ellie nodded, "Sounds familiar."

Morgan smiled some very nice teeth for a guy who formerly made a living fighting in the N.H.L. He got in the cruiser and drove away.

Chapter 11.

Questions at brunch

It was Sunday so Ellie and Mill walked to church in town and then had brunch at the Greek diner. Sitting at one of the booths by a big bay window looking out on Main Street was Roger Michter answering some of the questions on the sheets of paper Ellie had given him last night. He looked a little worn and in arrears in the sleep category.

"Ladies," he said with small smile. "How are you this morning? Ellie, I'm going through your questions, they really make you think."

"We've found them invaluable."

"It's hard to concentrate. I keep seeing that poor boy's face. The waiter. He's dead. Officer Morgan came to see me a few hours ago. Did you know? They found him in the park. I guess he was a drug addict."

"We know. Officer Morgan came to see us. Did you know him?"

"No, not in the slightest."

Ellie thought, *JWIII knew Skewed Hat and spoke to him at the town meeting as well as the party, and Roger Michter knows JWIII and was also at the town meeting and party. Seemed a little too close for comfort.* She blurted out, "Doesn't James Winnington III know him? I saw them. Together. Twice."

Michter looked confused, "When?"

"At the town meeting yesterday and then at the party."

"Winnington was at the meeting on the dais with me. Didn't you see him?"

"Yes, I know, but he left and went out in the anteroom of the gym to speak to the now dead waiter. They were speaking together at the party last night as well."

"I remember Winnington getting up for a few minutes from the dais at the town meeting, he said he was going to the bathroom. What were they talking about when you saw them?"

"I don't know. I couldn't hear them."

Michter looked out of the big bay window of the diner, sighed, and said, "I'll have to ask him about it. I don't know this person with a skewed hat save for an informal hello before the party got started. Did you ask Winnington if he knew him? Did the police ask him?"

Mill chimed in, "Roger, it is 11:30 Sunday morning and we're just back from church. We have not been out looking for James Winnington III, though the police say they are looking for him."

If on cue, Officer Morgan appeared and walked over to the booth they were sitting at. "I saw you all in here and thought I would say hello."

"Did you find Winnington?" asked Ellie.

"Indeed, I did." He was driving a red MG and was right across from me at the Main Street traffic light not terribly far from Ms. Mill's house. Morgan had just a hint of a Canadian accent, so *house* came out like *hoos*.

"And what happened?" asked Mill.

"I hit my lights, and he looked around to see if anyone else was in the intersection except for us, saw there wasn't, and for about three seconds as I was making a U-turn, he floored it to start to get away, then stopped, pulled over and was as nice as you please."

"What did he say about the waiter? The guy with the skewed hat?"

His words exactly were—and he imitated an affected Wall Street voice, "What guy with a skewed hat? What waiter? I don't specifically remember what the waiter looked like. I thought all the caterer's waiters were women, come to think of it."

"You've got to be kidding," Ellie said. "That's it?"

"He swore up and down," Morgan said cynically.

"But you saw him talking to the guy in the skewed hat at the Town Meeting, right?"

"No, I'm sorry. I only saw you two in the ladies room because that woman and her kid were trying to get in and it was locked."

"But you had to have seen them together!" Ellie pleaded.

"No, I just saw you trying to get out of the ladies room and him on the floor."

Michter took notice of that and asked, "What's that all about? Is there something between you and Winnington romantically?"

"No!" Ellie nearly yelled. Most of the eyes of the diner were already on the policeman and Mill's tall granddaughter who—everyone in town knew by now—had slugged that nice, new, and very handsome policeman who used to play hockey at the town meeting yesterday after she was having a torrid romantic interlude in the high school gym ladies room with one of those hotel people even though she has a serious boyfriend in the city.

"I'm sorry," Morgan repeated. I didn't see.

"Where did Winnington get his car?" Ellie asked.

"What?" Morgan asked, confused.

"He flew out here with me on the seaplane in a three-piece suit and a briefcase. No luggage. I was the only one on the plane Friday that stowed luggage. Where did he get a car? Where did he get his clothes? The nearest place to rent a car is thirty minutes from here at least. He didn't wear a three-piece suit at the town meeting yesterday."

Morgan opened a little three by five spiral notebook he kept in his left pocket with a tiny pencil tucked in the spiral and made a note. "I'll check."

Morgan asked Michter, "How long have you known James Winnington III?"

"He's an investment banker that we work with. He has a specialty in real estate. He's been extraordinarily successful ever since he got out of school. He's done dozens upon dozens of deals—most of them in the last five years. Everything he touches turns to gold. He gets the folks who need money to build something, like what I'm trying to do in Sounion and matches them up with people who have money, or want to merge."

Mill asked, "But you're not trying to merge."

"No," said Michter. "It's a straight dollar deal if you will."

"And who is his funder? Where's the money coming from?"

"It's a multi-national conglomerate of some banks, high net worth individuals, and some endowment funds, but essentially, the funder is one man—a very secretive man." With pride Michter added, "He's coming here tomorrow."

"What's his name?"

"Beckwith Chambers. He's British. People say he was the reason Maggie Thatcher won in '79. Shuns publicity except for when a charity he supports asks him for a photo op. If anything reaches the papers about him, the deal's off. We've done a half dozen projects with him. Took us forever to do due diligence on him at first because there was very little about him."

Morgan asked, "What does 'due diligence' mean?"

"Oh, sorry. 'Due diligence' is a background and financial audit of a person so you can clear them to be a business partner.

"And did he clear?"

"Yes, his books were pristine. Our lawyer, Morris Barkwell, handled the audit personally and if Morris can't find anything, then you're clean. We plan to be doing a lot more deals with him. It's all thanks to James Winnington III." He looked over at Ellie with a look of concern, "Ellie, Winnington is a bit full of himself I'll admit because of all his success, but he's a very hard worker and I've never had the slightest trouble with him. You don't need to ask so many questions about him." He said it as if that ended the Winnington topic once and for all.

Jessica Traverts, the caterer from last night's party and Michter's girlfriend came in. She walked right over to Officer Morgan, who by this time had sat down at the booth with Michter, Mill, and Ellie. Jessica asked, "Any leads?"

"No."

"That poor boy," she said forlornly.

"Ellie seems to think that there's a connection between Winnington and the boy who died. She's been asking a lot of questions." Michter said as Traverts sat.

"Did you know his name?" Morgan asked her.

"No, I tend to just pay first-timers out of petty cash so they don't have to pay taxes. It was Ricky something. He said it really fast when he showed up to help out," she said

"You never met him before?"

"No, this party," she smiled over at Roger Michter. The party was put together so fast, it made my head spin. And, it's Memorial Day weekend, so I gave a lot of my staff off because next week, we get crazy busy.

"How did you hire him?" Ellie asked.

"I put up little eight-and-a-half by eleven sheets of paper with tabs on them to call me—out where we-uh, Roger is renting."

"And he called."

"Sure, I pay well and it's an easy gig. He came early and stayed late. I just didn't catch his last name. He was doing such a good job, I asked if he would work at a huge event we're doing in the Hamptons next weekend for some Hollywood producers. I told him to call me on Sunday, which would've been today, to let me know his Social Security number and how to spell his name. I knew I couldn't do petty cash forever."

Mayor Archie Richardson came in. Ellie and Mill had seen him at church a little while ago. He came over and shook hands with Michter. "I hear your funder is coming in tomorrow. How is he getting here?"

Michter said, "He told me he wants the true Sounion experience. He was going to take a rented chopper out and land it on the football field, but thought that would be over the top, so he—you won't believe what he asked," Michter took on a British accent, "'Say chap, I don't want to die of old age in these massive traffic jams I hear about across the pond. Got an alternative to loud choppers and slow traffic?"

"I told him about the seaplane."

"Ha!" laughed Mayor Richardson. "A guy worth all that money taking the little dinky four-seater out here? Has he made a reservation with Mac the Pilot?"

"He told me to book all the seats so he doesn't have to speak to anyone. I told Mac when I made the reservation that he's a little eccentric."

"Mac's going to be all right with him right up front?"

"He better be."

Everyone had brunch, Michter gave Ellie the answers to her questions, and she promised she would start on them that afternoon.

"I like your service! Working on a Sunday afternoon."

"It's just to get familiar with the project."

When she got back to her little place above Ellie's garage, she drew a new person on her list, *Beckwith Chambers*, and drew a Union Jack above his name.

Chapter 12.

A question in particular

Ellie went up to her room above Mill's garage and started to work on some logo sketches. She had a fax machine where she faxed all the answers to her office with a note that she would just work out in Sounion and wouldn't be in the office next week. Several other staffers took the week off after Memorial Day so she thought she could get some sun, some work done, and maybe figure out what was going on in Sounion. The last item had begun to take over more and more of her thoughts.

She worked throughout the day studying Michter's answers about his company and his preferences about logos.

Most of the afternoon was spent sketching logos: She made notes about what fonts to use on the logo. She went on to make several small icons for a hotel, the seaside, and even a few with a seaplane because one of Michter's answers to the "amenities" of the hotel was, "Charter a seaplane to see the coast or to whisk you into Manhattan for dinner and the theater!" Ellie thought the seaplane could be an out-of-the-box solution to the logo.

The afternoon went by quickly and around five, she smelled chicken and vegetables grilling out on Mill's back deck. She knew dinner was about twenty minutes away, so she placed a call to her assistant Bobby who lived a couple of blocks from the office. Bobby was a Tasmanian Devil of activity and was always saying, "Boss, if you need something over the weekend, you call me, and I'll do it."

Ellie never took him up on it since she'd been named President of the firm—until this afternoon. He picked up on the first ring. "Were you expecting a call?"

"No, Boss. Answering after the first ring is a sign of weakness."

She smiled because he was always taking mundane things and adding the phrase, "is a sign of weakness." Last week it was "Drinking skim milk is a sign of weakness." The week before that it was, "Taking taxis, except to the airport, is a sign of weakness."

"Can you do a quick thing for me?" Ellie asked.

Bobby, approaching Nirvana at the opportunity said, "It's go time. Tell me, Boss." He said it like he was locking and loading for Omaha Beach.

"Can you go to the office and put my 'Current Projects' folder in a large envelope and have that messenger service that does weekends and holiday deliveries—"

He interrupted, "Anytime-Anywhere Messengers. They have those cool checkerboard baseball hats with orange polo shirts."

"Right, that's the one. Can you have one of their messengers drop it off here at my grandmother's place. I'm guessing they'll have several packages out past Sounion to the Hamptons tomorrow."

She gave him her grandmother's address.

"I'm on it. They guarantee delivery between ten and noon on the holiday if picked up before eight in the morning and I'll make sure it's done. You can count on me. I'll be in the office all week answering phones, Boss. I'll talk to you later. I'm going over to the office right now."

And he rung off.

Ellie walked down and around to the deck of the main house where Mill was grilling. Mill had on Wayfarers as the sun was getting low on the horizon, cargo shorts, a white linen top, a Cowdray pearl necklace, and Birkenstocks. She once heard Mill quote Coco Chanel, "A woman needs ropes and ropes of pearls."

"Smells good," Ellie said.

"I got the chicken and vegetables at the farmer's market in town this afternoon. There aren't many farmers left on the island and certainly not so many around Sounion. I can remember when this was mostly potato fields. I will say, it's the best chicken I've ever had." Her attention went back to her grilling and she nonchalantly said, "And your mother called."

Ellie raised an eyebrow in response.

Mill poked a sliced cucumber on the grill and said, "She didn't say hello, she just asked, 'Am I too hard on her?'"

"And you said?"

"You know how it is with your mother, the answer lies in how you answer."

"Then, how did you answer?"

"With a question."

"What was the question?"

"I said, 'Daughter, has it ever occurred to you that your daughter is likely at the top of heap in the most competitive design environment on the planet? Loves you unconditionally, no matter how you treat her, and that your husband wouldn't give your daughter the silent treatment even if she was at the bottom of the heap? *Wrapping paper? Really, Daughter?*'"

Ellie smiled, "If I said that, she'd really not speak to me."

Continuing on, Mill said, "And, don't you think that at the age of thirty-three, your daughter may one day stop trying to deal with you and cut you off completely? She could get a job in any big city in the world. She could just leave New York and maybe take a job in London and never come back.'"

"Gracious, how did she answer that?"

Mill turned, looked at her, and channeled her own daughter's distinctive hoarse voice to her granddaughter, "Mother, don't you know I worry about that every single damn day of my life." She poked at the chicken some more, "That's the gospel truth. And she hung up."

"Well, that's something."

Mill chuckled, "Then again, she may not be speaking to me now!"

Ellie looked out into the ocean, she was thinking back when she was in high school and graduated third in her class at the most prestigious private school in Manhattan. She had a special affinity for Biology. She'd smoked the A.P. Bio test and won an impressive award at a weekend conclave of high school Bio whizzes in Boston. Her mother was so proud of her, confident she was going to medical school, she'd introduce her at parties—much to Ellie's chagrin—as *Young Doctor Ellie*. Dr. Pincrest had told her only child that her only real choice was to go to Brown, in Providence, Rhode Island as she had done.

Ellie's response a few weeks before Christmas of her senior year in high school was to tell her mother that she would indeed be going to school in Providence, Rhode Island, but at the Rhode Island School of Design, considered by many to be the best design school in the nation specifically to study logo design. She did not want to be a doctor—and had never wanted to become a doctor. Ever. What she didn't say out loud is she was terrified of becoming her mother.

Dr. Pincrest laughed as she thought her daughter had just told a witty off-the-cuff joke, but Ellie's hopeful face told a different story. Dr. Pincrest and Ellie got into another fight for the ages. During the screaming match, where Dr. Pincrest had vowed to cut off Ellie without one red cent for college unless she went to Brown, to which Ellie countered that her portfolio of high school work had secured her a full scholarship, the phone rang and it was Ellie's father calling from a recording session in Los Angeles. Ellie picked up with Ellie's mom screaming in the background. The only words he said were, "I'll stop the recording session right now and take the red eye back in two hours. I'll see you two in the morning and broker some kind of peace agreement."

Looking out at the ocean, Ellie said, "Sometimes, I think I may have had enough of Mom,"

Mill chuckled mischievously, "Changing the subject slightly, I got ahold of that *Playboy*."

"Oh, Grandma. You are truly out of your mind." Ellie tilted her head slightly, "So, what does the woman who stole my man look like?"

"Lots of airbrushing," Mill said in the most concerned face she could muster as she whipped the *Playboy* out of her cargo shorts side pocket and showed Ellie the centerfold. Mill held the faux concerned face for a few seconds and then burst out laughing.

Ellie and Mill laughed until they needed an oxygen hook-up. Ellie finally hacked out, "Oh, Grandma, you know she's gorgeous for heaven's sake!"

They ate and looked at the sun slipping down on the horizon when Mill said, "What's up with this Roger Michter? Something's going on there."

"Join the club. I've been thinking about it all afternoon. At the Greek diner, I had questions about James Winnington's suddenly having a car and clothes. When I flew out with him, he said he had neither."

"And no place to stay, right? He said that on the dock."

"And no place to stay," Ellie repeated.

"Michter certainly didn't say anything about it. If they were such close business associates, you would think that he would know more."

"It may sound a little crazy, but since I'm working on this and I'm a little uneasy, I have a few more questions for Roger Michter about James Winnington III."

"Are you calling? Or are we driving over?"

"What's this *we* stuff?" Ellie said.

"You can't drive, remember?"

"Bringing up pertinent details again, I see."

"It's a grandmother's job."

"Let me ring him up and tell him we're coming over."

"I'll get a wrap; it's getting a little chilly. Then I'll pull the car around."

Ellie walked up to her room and dialed Michter's number that he'd put on the back of his business card. He answered on the fourth ring and Ellie smiled wondering if her assistant would think it was a sign of weakness, "Hello?"

"Roger, hi. Ellie Pincrest. I have a couple of follow up questions on your answers today. It's such a nice night out and my grandmother and I were going to take a little spin just to get some night air. Would you mind if we came by for a few minutes? I hope it's not too much of an intrusion."

He was tickled, "Absolutely, come on by. We're just watching the Mets game. They're in first place!"

"We'll be by in a few minutes."

Ellie got in the Karman-Ghia with Mill at the wheel and they drove over to Michter's place. He answered the door wearing his usual khakis, no socks, loafers, and oxford shirt. "Ladies, a pleasure. Come in-come in."

Jessica peeked her head around the corner and waved, "I'm just finishing up with some dishes, you all go into the Roger's den and chat."

"First place. The Mets! Can you believe it?" Roger said.

"I'm not much of a baseball fan, though I have been to Shea Stadium several times over the years with clients in those box things where they serve drinks and food."

"Ah, a *Luxury Box*."

"That's it. Roger, we're sorry to intrude on your down time, but I've got three or four questions on your answers from earlier today."

Ellie adroitly made up several questions on the fly hoping to steer the conversation in such a manner where Michter would be forced to say, "Let me find out from Winnington."

He did exactly that on her last question. While she made a note, she offhandedly asked, "Speaking of Winnington, I rode out in the seaplane with him. Does he have a place out here and a car? He was saying he didn't even have clothes out here."

"I got them for him." It was Jessica, drying her hands on a dish towel. "He said he wanted to stay out here, so I volunteered to get him some clothes and rent a car for him. I just went to one of those rent-a-wreck-for-a-week things. Winnington gave me money and told me kind of abruptly to find one. Actually, he was rude about it. Even arranged a house rental for him, he barely said thanks." She waved a goodnight to everyone and went upstairs in the big house.

"Isn't she a peach? I've been so busy she didn't even want to bother me with that detail." Michter said proudly.

Ellie nodded, but acted like she was looking for more questions on her sheets. "Well, that's all my questions."

Roger said excitedly, "Hey, Beckwith Chambers is coming in on the nine o'clock seaplane tomorrow morning. Ellie, why don't you meet him at dock? I'll be there."

"He'd want to meet me?" Ellie asked.

"Of course he would! And it'll be a perfect opportunity for you to get a bit of his vision. It's intriguing. He kind of draws you in. He seems to know what you're thinking before you say it."

Ellie said, "I'd love to. It's not every day a billionaire comes to Sounion."

Mill asked two more off-the-cuff questions, shook hands with Roger and she and Mill drove home.

As they pulled into the driveway, Mill said, "Maybe I should write a mystery novel and give it the title, *A Billionaire Comes to Sounion.*"

Chapter 13.

The billionaire and the messenger

At precisely nine the next morning, Ellie heard the drone of Mac the Pilot's seaplane engine change as he began his descent toward Sounion. She stood on the dock and looked up in the sky as he banked and extended his flaps for his water landing. It wasn't until she was walking on to the dock that she thought that James Winnington III could be there as well.

She took her eyes off the plane and looked around for him. She feared he might push her into the water and hold her under.

"Where's Winnington?" she asked Roger Michter who was standing nearby, actually pacing a bit anxiously, reciting some finance figures he'd memorized overnight. Jessica Traverts was there for moral support. Mayor Richardson was in tow as well. Ellie wondered why the high school marching band had not been requested to play *God Save the Queen*.

The plane landed perfectly; Mac's landings were always perfect. He taxied over to the dock. Mac did some fancy footwork to get out of the plane and on to a pontoon to secure his aircraft to the dock.

And, out came Beckwith Chambers.

Short. Very, as so many of the super rich are. About fiftyish. Sandy blonde hair, swept back. He'd swept it back twice within five steps on the dock. Stylish sunglasses, hence, she couldn't see the color of his eyes. Neat jeans with an open collar shirt and a well-tailored almond-color suit jacket. He was looking around to get a measure of the place. He saw Michter, smiled, and nodded him over.

Michter, anxious beyond belief almost tripped over himself walking over. He recovered and said obsequiously, "Beckwith, Beckwith. So glad to see you!"

Beckwith Chambers spoke with a deep, rich British voice. If they had Beefeater Gin commercials on television, Chambers would be a very satisfying choice as voiceover man, "Roger, my dear friend. It's been too long. Maybe some golf later today, shall we? I've got some ideas that I'm failing to keep inside me!"

"At the earliest-at the earliest!" Roger exclaimed. "You remember Jessica Traverts, caterer extraordinaire."

"How could I ever forget anyone so lovely?"

"And this is the mayor of Sounion, Mayor Archie Richardson."

"Oh, ha! Like Archie Leach! Did you know, old man, that was Cary Grant's real name?"

Mayor Richardson didn't know what to do with a billionaire talking to him about Cary Grant. "Uh, well. No, actually. I did not," he smiled.

"A little movie trivia for you: He mentions his real name in *His Girl Friday*. I wonder if Grant improvised it on the spot!"

Beckwith Chambers looked over at Ellie and extended his hand, "And this must be the logo developer. I hear you're actually *from* Sounion."

"Hello, Mr. Chambers, I'm Ellie Pincrest. My grandmother lives here, I was born and raised in Manhattan. I have a little room above her garage."

Chambers came back quickly with, "Blimey! Let's hope you weren't put above the garage for misbehaving in your grandmother's house!"

Everyone laughed because everyone had a vested interest in moving out all the anxiety. Michter looked like he was going to laugh and throw up at the same time. His suave demeanor had been replaced by a grim obsequiousness in the presence of his money pipeline in the flesh.

There was small talk for several minutes between Chambers and Michter. Ellie saw that Jessica wasn't speaking to anyone; kind of lost in her own thoughts, so she walked over.

"How long have you known Roger?" Ellie asked.

"About five years. He used my catering firm on several occasions. We always chatted after." Quietly so Roger and Beckwith couldn't hear, she said, "And that turned into some unabashed flirting, and that turned into him making a successful pass at me very late after a party clean-up. He's been pretty wonderful to me to say the least."

Roger and Beckwith turned around and Beckwith said, "Gracious, me. Look how inconsiderate I am, not talking to everyone at once. What say we go into town and have some tea and do some chatting?"

There were smiles all around, but Ellie said, "May I have a raincheck, Mr. Chambers? I'm expecting a messenger at my house between ten and noon and I really should be there for him."

He reached out and shook her hand, "My dear, only if from now on you call me, 'Beckwith.'"

Ellie smiled and said, "Of course, Beckwith. I apologize. I didn't know I would be going with all of you."

"No need for apologies, my dear. I'm sure we'll be chatting quite a lot over the next few days."

As a group, they turned and walked up toward Main Street and turned right, likely headed for the Greek diner. Ellie turned left and walked back to Mill's place and her room.

At ten thirty, Ellie was coming out of the bathroom when she heard a van roll into the driveway. She looked out the window of her room and saw the van driver wearing the distinctive checkerboard baseball hat with orange polo shirt. He was inside a van with *Anytime-Anywhere Messengers* stenciled in italicized aqua blue Bodoni font. Ellie could identify any font instantly. Her level of font recall shook up her staff. Several junior staffers over the years had studied and studied trying to keep up with her in meetings with clients, but they all failed. Once in the Ladies Room at the office, two junior staffers, not knowing Ellie was in one of the stalls said her instant recall of any font ever created was "Savant-like."

And then something strange happened.

The messenger got out of the van and just bounded up the stairs.

He didn't go to the main house, he didn't linger to see if someone was going to come out and get him, he went right to Ellie's stairs and bounded right up. *How did he know to come to a door above a garage at a house he'd never been to in his life?*

Ellie opened the door just as he got to the top.

"How did—" she tried to say.

"Hello!" said a large man too loudly and too friendly in a way too small shirt. He didn't even bother to button the top three buttons and the checkboard hat was kind of stuck on his large head. "I have a package for Ellie." He said it really fast.

"Yes, that's me—"

He pushed past her and went into her room and said, "I don't have a pen and I need you to sign for this Ellie. Do you have a pen, Ellie?"

Ellie was about to tell him to get the blazes out of her room when he made a quick motion, turned around and slammed the door shut. Worse, his big smile and loudness vanished. It was replaced with a sinister and low, "So, I think it's time you went back to Manhattan and stopped hanging around Sounion."

"Who the Sam Hill are you?"

"Just a simple messenger delivering a simple message." He moved closer to her and was angling her toward a sofa near the door.

"How did you know I lived up here?!"

"Oh, I know a lot of things, the most important thing is you ask a lot of questions about people, about hotels, about Sounion. Maybe it's time to go back to Manhattan." He pushed her on to the sofa.

Ellie screamed bloody murder—which was exactly what she was worried the result of this encounter was going to be if she didn't do something quick—and she thrust up her knee in the same motion she did on James Winnington in the Ladies Room at the gym, but the messenger was quick to deflect it with his tree trunk of a leg. "Oh, I like a spirited girl." Then he frowned menacingly and said, "But not too spirited," and he pushed her back on the sofa and clamped his hand over her mouth. Ellie tried to get free, but he was simply too large and muscular.

Suddenly, he flew off of her as if she had an electric force field running through her.

Claude Morgan had grabbed the messenger by the back of his pants and hurled him off. The Messenger slid down on his butt, looked up and saw it was a policeman, smiled malignantly, and said to Morgan, "Oh, I'm going to put all sorts of hurt on you, cop."

The messenger could not have been more wrong.

Morgan let the messenger up motioning him to come closer and did two things at once: He grabbed both sides of the messenger's too small shirt, pulled it quickly up and then over his head. Ellie seemed to remember seeing a hockey fight one night with her ex at Madison Square Garden and this is exactly what happened. One player picked a fight with another, and the other player pulled his jersey (Ellie swore they called them *"sweaters,"* ironically.) and started whaling away.

The messenger was flailing blindly with his arms as Morgan delivered three quick punches to the messenger's solar plexus. As it spasmed, the messenger couldn't catch his breath and fell to the floor in a heap.

Morgan stood over him and in a dry voice (and not breathing hard Ellie noted) said to the messenger, "Didn't catch what you said to me before?"

The messenger had managed to get the shirt off of his head as he lay on the floor, but he was making little "o" shapes with his mouth trying to get air in. Morgan stood over him and said, "Breathe, sir. You'll be alright in a minute."

The messenger responded by trying to punch Morgan from a sitting position on the floor, but Morgan literally caught the fist of the messenger in his hand like a weakly hit ground ball. Morgan squeezed. Hard. The messenger yelped. It sounded like a small dog barking backwards.

Morgan asked, "Who are you?"

In a breathless voice, the messenger told Morgan what he could do with himself.

It was the wrong answer and now Morgan squeezed and twisted and said, "I saw you on top of this woman who was screaming for help."

"It was consensual," he said trying to get more air in his lungs.

"Again with that?! What is it with you men?" Ellie exclaimed and grabbed an X-Acto knife off her drafting table and held it up in front of her with two hands.

"You have no idea who you're dealing with!"

Dryly again, Morgan said, "I've dealt with you without too much trouble."

The messenger seemed stuck on his same response because he told Morgan again what he could do with himself.

Mill appeared in the doorway and said, "Who the hell is this?!"

Ellie said, "This man tried to threaten me and told me to go back to Manhattan, that I was asking too many questions, and to get out of Sounion. He then he tried to rape me."

Mill put her hand over her heart, withdrew it and savagely slugged the messenger right in his right occipital bone. Ellie heard a crack and hoped it was the messenger's bone and not Mill's hand.

"Grandma!" she cried.

Ignoring Ellie and only focusing on the messenger, she said, "If you ever get out of prison, I will find you and I will kill you."

Morgan looked at Ellie. Ellie had so much adrenaline coursing through her she didn't know what to say.

"How long have you worked at the messenger service?" Morgan asked.

"You really think I work for a messenger service?"

Morgan took out the cuffs, forcibly put the messenger's arms behind him, and put on the cuffs. As they started walking to the door, the messenger shook free and at the landing at the top of the stairs, tried to scissor kick over the railing and on to the driveway to get away, but his trail leg caught and it turned him headfirst and down. With no hands to catch him, he dropped to the driveway, his forehead hitting first, sixteen feet below and snapped his neck.

The messenger was dead.

Morgan, Mill, and Ellie scrambled down the stairs, Morgan immediately radioed in for an ambulance and back-up. Since Mill didn't live too far from Main Street, she heard the E.M.T. truck fire up right away and turn on its siren. Two minutes later, they heard the police back-up coming.

It was no use. There was a frothy red substance coming out of the messenger's mouth. He was a goner.

A banging noise came from the van with a muffled cry for help. Morgan opened the back of the van and a shirtless messenger tumbled out of the back. He was tied up with packing tape around his wrists and ankles and had a huge wad of packing tape stuffed in his mouth. Morgan freed him and the real messenger—who was quite a bit smaller than the false messenger—yelled, "A guy carjacked my van when I stopped for coffee this morning on the expressway! Where is he? Where is he?"

When the real messenger looked over and saw his clothes on a dead man, he got very rubber-legged and slumped against the van. Mill and Ellie helped him as the ambulance came in and an E.M.T.s got out and rushed over to the faux messenger.

"What happened?" he yelled.

"He tried to escape and jump over the railing from the top. He went headfirst into the driveway," Morgan said. Ellie thought that if this weren't such a tragic scene, the way he said it, would've sounded like a punchline in a movie. But, when she looked over at Morgan, he wasn't laughing. He was clearly shaken. This had gone badly. And when his police captain, who just happened to be police back-up this Memorial Day morning, showed up, Ellie knew that Claude Morgan was in for it.

The captain for Sounion was even bigger and fitter than Morgan. He was about 50, had salt-and-pepper hair and a U.S.M.C. tattoo on his left bicep. They spoke for several minutes. You couldn't really hear what Morgan was saying, but clear as a bell you could hear every one of the captain's, "You idiot!" and "Are you kidding me?!" and "How stupid are you?!"

Ellie got incensed enough that she walked over and tapped the Captain on the shoulder. He spun around and barked, "What is it? Can't you see I'm busy here?!"

"Aren't you interested in hearing from the victim?" she said.

He snarled, "The only victim I see is a dead guy about twenty feet from us."

Ellie didn't back down, "Well, does it interest you to know I was about to be raped and Officer Morgan likely saved my life?"

The Captain glared at her, and caught himself. He shifted his glance over to Mill who was standing off to the side. Ellie heard her say, "Bob, maybe you should take my granddaughter's statement. She's quite lucky to be alive—thanks to Claude." The captain did as Mill suggested.

As she was giving her statement, Ellie realized that someone was listening in on her phone calls.

Chapter 14.

Did he go blind?

The captain calmed down and by the time he left, he'd even smiled at Morgan and patted him on the arm.

"You alright?" Ellie asked him.

"Shouldn't I be asking you that?" Morgan said.

"Look, Officer Morgan," Ellie started.

"You can call me 'Claude' if you wish." He turned to look at the departing police car. "Maybe not around the captain, though. I'm in his *Chateau Bow-Wow* right now."

Ellie smiled, "Okay, 'Claude.' That's such a French sounding name."

"At least one male on my mother's side has been named Claude since the 1700s."

"Claude, I think my phone's been tapped."

"Wow, you come out to Sounion and all manner of disaster follows. Why do you think you're bugged?"

"That false messenger, he went right up to my door. No hesitation. He didn't go to the main house. He *knew* where to find me. He knew what messenger service was bringing out the package to me. The false messenger tracked him and just took his place."

"You called the messenger service yourself?"

"No, I called my assistant and my assistant set it up."

Morgan looked over at the spot where the false messenger had landed. There was still a blood stain. "I have a friend who can help us. I won't have to submit any paperwork to the department for budget authorization; he'll do it for a friend."

"He'll see if my phone is tapped?"

"Yes."

Ellie groaned. "Who would want to tap my phone?!"

"This false messenger said, that you 'ask a lot of questions.' That means that someone associated with the hotel people, or their money funders, or someone with the town is displeased with you. Maybe someone with the hotel is thinking you're going to stir things up. Maybe someone in town sees you as an outsider stirring things up."

"They literally are my client! Why would want to hurt my client! On the other side, I've been coming here for over three decades! I know most everyone in town!"

"Maybe someone with the money funders."

"James Winnington III?"

"Seems somewhat likely. All of your questions are directed at him. On the town side, could be two factions that are potentially displeased with you." He was trying to be sensitive and calm her down a little, but it wasn't working. "The two factions are: Those folks who absolutely don't want a luxury hotel in Sounion. You're seen as the person helping them. The other faction are those people who absolutely want a luxury hotel in Sounion and you're hurting them."

Ellie put her head in her hands. "Wasn't it enough that I got dumped? Why am I also being attacked?"

"What?"

"Several days ago, my longtime boyfriend dumped me."

Flatly, Claude asked, "Did he go blind?"

"What?"

"Did he go blind?"

"What are you talking about?"

"A man would have to be cra-. Nevermind."

"He got married to someone else on Friday and they are in Paris at this very moment on their honeymoon."

"And you wanted to marry a guy that would do that to another human being?"

"I didn't really think about being married to him, we were always just together."

"*Together* and *married* are two very different things."

"You're a therapist now?"

"When you're a cop, you're a lot of things."

For some reason, that miffed Ellie. "Am I so predictable? Or, are you saying I was just too wrapped up in my own career that I couldn't see what was going on right in front of me? Or, are you saying that I just wasn't worth it to him?" she said, not really speaking to Officer Claude Morgan of the Sounion Cove police department, but to the last five years of her life.

Morgan still felt badly. "I'm sorry. Maybe I was a little too quick to opine."

She turned and started walking up to her room. Over her shoulder, she said, "Thanks for the 'blindness' compliment. I'm sure you were sincere." It came out like she was saying goodbye.

As she got to the stop of the stairs, he said, "I'll call my friend and he'll look at your phone."

She didn't respond.

She closed the door and started packing to go back to Manhattan.

Chapter 15.

Packing to go home

Ellie was sitting on her bed, fighting off tears when there was a gentle knock. "You there, sweetie?" It was Mill.

Ellie opened the door and there was Mill in oversized pink clown sunglasses that had a little flamingo in the bridge. Ellie looked at her and said solemnly, "How are you and my mother even from the same water supply?"

"Divine intervention," Mill said.

"I'm going to go back to Manhattan. The need to get away to Sounion has been suppressed by two dead people, punching a cop, the whole town thinking I had sex with a guy in the gym bathroom, a messenger attacking me, and oh, him being dead too. Three dead people."

"That's quite a lineup."

Ellie walked over to her bureau, opened a drawer, pulled out a couple of bras and put tossed them haphazardly somewhat near the overnight bag in the middle of the floor. "What's funny, I don't think about Stephen. My ex. I got here and things just started happening. I should've never gotten on that seaplane."

"Two things: First, you should always visit your grandmother, so you should've definitely gotten on that plane. Second, you've walked into something out here, but you'll obsess and obsess about it until you figure it out. And it will gnaw at you if you're back in Manhattan—you'll feel helpless. It's the one thing you share in common with your mother, when you two sink your teeth into something, you don't let go."

"I seemed to let Stephen go."

"You held on to him and *he* decided to go. *He* seems to have put together some kind of palace in his head where his queen needs to sit and she has to fill several requirements. My prediction on that marriage is that the first moment she sprouts a wrinkle or crow's feet or sags, he'll be out the door."

"Everyone's a therapist around me today," she said blankly.

"Stephen being in Paris and married to another woman is very, very likely the best thing that ever happened to you. Do you really think he was going to let you keep working after you were married and had children?"

"Maybe I wanted to not work after I got married and had children. I hadn't really thought about it."

"My point is that *Stephen* would resent *him* not making the decision for you. Admit it, I'm right. He wanted total control. And, let's face it, he has always been jealous of your success."

Over the next few minutes as she stared at her open bag, Ellie evaluated several dozen pieces of evidence regarding Stephen—scraps of conversations, arguments, notes, phone calls, dinners, and remarks from over the past five years. She sighed and said, "You're right."

In a diffident tone, Mill asked, "Would you do me a favor and stay for the Memorial Day parade? Men of all ages, especially the college kids back from school, hit on me at the parade, and I'm going to need protection. It's super awkward. I don't want to be part of any village scandal." A few quiet moments passed and then she burst out laughing as Ellie stood there shaking her head and rolling her eyes. Mill started putting Ellie's things back in her drawers and put her bag away to stay for the rest of the week.

Ellie and Mill walked over to the parade route on Main Street. You could feel the excitement of people, floats, marching bands, Little League teams, Shriners on motor scooters, and, of course, veterans of all ages. Several World War I veterans were still going strong and even they were walking in the parade.

Ellie had spent every Memorial Day (save for that summer abroad junior year in Florence) in Sounion and two things were rock solid guarantees: One, it would be blazing hot and humid by nine in the morning. And two, by three in the afternoon, the skies would turn the blackest black, toad strangle rain for twenty minutes with Wagnerian thunder and lightning, and the Sun would be out by five with everyone having lobsters and corn on the cob.

Several towns' people stopped to talk to Mill or she stopped them. There was a lot of laughing, hugging, and *My have you grown since last years.* Mill knew all the veterans in town. She also knew all of the widows and mothers in town of the soldiers who went to places like Saint Mihiel, Anzio, Guadalcanal, Imjin River, Khe Sanh, and did not come back. That's who they were memorializing today.

Mill said as they got to the parade route on Main Street, "When I was a little girl, I talked to two men who'd fought at Gettysburg. One fought for the Union and the other for the Confederacy. They were great friends and had a small law firm on Main Street. They both lived to be one hundred. They called Memorial Day by its original name, 'Decoration Day.'"

A line of baton twirling majorettes led the parade down Main Street followed by the high school marching band. Several of the car dealerships showed off their latest models, especially pick-up trucks that were easy to haul around local dignitaries. There were several floats that shed tissue paper like delicate petals from a flower.

Ellie and Mill were commenting about how great this year's parade was when they saw a vintage pick-up truck with a painted "Sounion By-the-Sea" sign on it with a subtitle, "A new paradigm in luxury hotels." There were equal number of cheers and boos as it went by. Ellie saw Morris Barkwell across the street watching the parade along with James Winnington III. They were watching Beckwith Chambers, Roger Michter, and Mayor Richardson ride down the street in the vintage pick-up.

A World War II P-51 fighter airplane made several swoops and buzzed Main Street making the throngs ooh and aah. The big bank clock clicked exactly twelve-twenty, when Ellie saw three junior high kids take a few steps out of the crowd, each light a twenty-four pack of firecrackers and toss them into the middle of the street. They went off and everyone did a quick flinch, but the familiar timbre of a firecracker didn't seem to bother most folks except everyone putting their fingers in their ears, and closing their eyes.

When Ellie opened her eyes, she saw that Mayor Richardson was holding his left shoulder, and Michter and Chambers were tending to him and asking if he was all right. There was a lot of smoke and it was difficult to see what was going on with all the parade noise, but Ellie yelled over to Mill, "I think there's something's wrong with Archie Richardson's arm."

Mill and Ellie walked down Main Street behind, tracking them. They started to run when they noticed that blood was staining Richardson's white shirt near the shoulder. "He's been shot!"

Claude Morgan had already jumped out into the parade route and was yelling instructions to the driver of the vintage pick-up, telling him to turn left at the next street for Mayor Richardson, who by now was laying down on the bed of the pick-up.

Mill and Ellie cut across the parade route and over to where the pick-up had pulled over and gone into the parking lot of the local grocery store. When they walked up, Ellie heard a hysterical Richardson yell, "Somebody shot me!"

Morgan had garnered an E.M.T., and he jumped up into the bed of the pick-up. Roger Michter's face was as ashen as Richardson's and Beckwith Chambers was looking like he was having a jolly good time—*these Americans!* Chambers, smiling broadly, leaned over to Michter and said in a loud voice, "Say, Yank. Is someone always getting shot at your parades?"

"Archie!" Mill yelled.

"Hi, Mill," he said breathlessly. "They got me."

"What does that mean?" Ellie asked.

Michter practically put his hand over Richardson's mouth. "He'll be okay, I think he's just a little delusional."

Richardson knocked his hands away, "You can't—" and he passed out for a few moments.

Morgan told the E.M.T. to get his ambulance over to the grocery store parking lot so they could load Richardson to get patched up at the local hospital.

The three boys who lit the firecrackers were being escorted by two large men, likely their fathers, as one had his grip firmly on the back on the neck of one boy and the other father had two boys—they looked like twins—one in each hand. They marched their juveniles over to the pick-up truck when Chambers jovially piped up again, "Looks like the parade is coming to the pick-up truck." Michter glared at him behind his back.

The fathers jerked their juveniles to stop, one was large, very football coach-ish looking with heavy-set everything, balding hair and an overgrown mustache. "Apologize! All of you! You wrecked the Memorial Day parade and injured Mayor Richardson who is a big supporter of our football program at the high school."

The three of them mumbled something that sounded like *Sawhuh* and they were promptly slapped upside the head by their fathers and instructed, "Do it *right*." The three corrected themselves and apologized as if they taught elocution classes.

Morgan asked, "Boys, where did you get the firecrackers? There usually aren't firecracker sales until June as we get closer to Fourth of July."

"Somebody gave them to us."

The other dad, who was even larger in height and girth than the football coach-ish dad squeezed his offending's son neck hard and said, "Liar!"

"Ow! Ow! Dad, I'm telling the truth. We were in the arcade about an hour ago playing Space Invaders and a guy walks up to us and says, "You kids want to have a good laugh at the parade today?"

"We weren't really paying attention to him so we said, 'Sure, whatever.' But then he threw the three packs firecrackers down on the Space Invaders console and said, 'I need you boys to do it exactly at twelve twenty, okay? It's important.'"

The dad let go of his son and said, "What else?"

"The guy threw down three fifty dollar bills and said, 'Fifty each for you. Just make sure twelve twenty.'"

Morgan asked, "Did you see him?"

Embarrassed, he said, pointing to the non-twin, "No, uh, you see, Tommy here was about to be all-time high score on Space Invaders and we were paying attention to that."

Morgan looked over at Tommy and said grimly, "Congratulations, kid."

Chapter 16.

Citizen's Arrest

The scene at the grocery store parking lot got surreal when James Winnington III himself showed up sporting a pink Ralph Lauren polo with the collar popped, white linen slacks, and escorting a man. Ellie couldn't remember the man's name offhand, "Bill-something" or other, the town drunk. Winnington had his hand clenched around Bill's forearm saying, "I've got him! Here's your man! Citizen's arrest!"

He triumphantly walked up to Officer Morgan and said, "Officer, I'd like to make a citizen's arrest of this man who fired a gun at our pick-up truck during the parade!" Winnington gave him a little push.

Over the years, Bill, the town drunk, had been arrested more times than a serial protestor. His nickname in town was "Otis Campbell" after the lovable Mayberry town drunk on *The Andy Griffith Show*. Women in town would bring him cherry pie when they knew he was locked up. Bill was the custodian/grass cutter at the high school and since he had never once been drunk while working and routinely put in extra hours while never once asking for overtime pay, the school administrators loved him.

It was Memorial Day, so Bill had had a few extra Long Island iced teas and was swaying a little bit. He said, "It was an accident! I swear!"

Winnington held up a kind of pip squeak, yet powerful enough to cause bleeding, pellet gun, "Here is the weapon in question."

Morgan looked at Winnington as if to say *You can't be serious.*

Winnington doubled-down, "Citizen's arrest! The streets need to be safe to have parades on. Especially after the hotel goes in!"

Morgan looked at Bill the town drunk and said, "Where'd you get the pellet gun, Bill?"

"Oh, you know, over by the, uh, where I live above the mechanic shop. I need one. Uh, mice. That's it! Got to, uh, keep them at, uh, bay. You know." Ellie caught Winnington slightly nodding his head for encouragement.

"And how did it go off?"

After perusing a short-list of lies in his head, Bill went with, "Didn't have the safety on." He held up Winnington's wrist and pointed first to the pellet gun that was a fraction of the size of a .45 and then to the safety on the left side of it.

"And then?"

"Well, I was fumbling around in my pocket, looking for some breath mints—you know how it is after a long night—and I still had this gun in my pocket from earlier this morning when some vermin were showing themselves—and when I pulled on the gun, I hit the trigger, and it went off."

Straining to keep the sarcasm out of his voice, Officer Morgan said, "You mean to tell me, on a crowded sidewalk during the biggest parade of the year, you reached for a gun at pocket level, accidentally fired it, the pellet made its way in between everyone standing in front of you on the parade route, and hit a moving target?"

At that moment, Mayor Archie Richardson jumped up like an Olympic gymnast who'd just stuck a landing and said in a hurried voice, "You know, I feel great. Just a scratch. Not even a flesh wound." He then started to mimic the *Monty Python* "Flesh Wound" routine and hopped around the bed of the pick-up. He thought he was hilarious, but everyone was just staring at him as if he was a few oars short of a boat.

He climbed out of the bed of the pick-up and turned to everyone, put his arms akimbo, touched the well-bandaged wound and said, "Feel great!" He bounded over to Bill and said sternly, "Now, Bill. I'm going to let this slide and not press charges because it was an accident. But, please. No more guns—even pellet guns—on our nice Main Street."

Morgan now looked at Richardson as if to say *You can't be serious.*

Richardson ignored him and walked off. Over his shoulder he said, "Have a nice Memorial Day everyone! Great weather for a cookout! Stop by our place at dinner time, we've got some delicious six pounders!"

Ellie, Mill, Richter, Chambers, the E.M.T., Winnington, Bill, the driver of the pick-up, the dads, the kids, and Morgan just watched him go. Morgan nodded his head and furrowed his eyebrow. His hand came up and then slapped hard against the pick-up, but didn't say anything else except, "Go. All of you."

Everyone scattered. Michter said, "I think I'll look for where my girlfriend has gone off to—hopefully still somewhere along the parade route or in one of the shops." He looked over at Chambers and said, now in a pleasant tone, "Beckwith, come with me. We'll find Jessica and then get our own cookout going over at the house."

Morgan's captain drove by and stopped to speak with him to make sure everyone was okay. He'd heard about the incident on the radio.

Ellie leaned over to Mill and said, "Let's take a walk."

And they set off to follow James Winnington III at a distance. He started off from the grocery store parking lot going down a little alley way. Ellie and Mill knew exactly where to go to both follow and hide. They noticed that Winnington went one way, then another, then doubled back. Very sneaky. He ended up at a cute little Craftsman-style house in a row of other cute little Craftsman-style houses. Ellie and Mill were able to follow him on a parallel street and look through the openings between houses. They hid behind a huge forsythia with its bright yellow early-summer flowers at the house across the street and prayed that the homeowners were at the parade.

Winnington walked up to the front stoop of the house, and sitting there, pretty as you please, was Jessica Traverts, *caterer extraordinaire*, with a big smile on her face. She put her arms around Winnington and kissed him passionately. He picked her up and spun her round and round as if she was a chair swing ride at a carnival. She squealed gleefully.

Mill dryly whispered to Ellie, "Well, at least she's seeing someone her own age."

Jessica and Winnington went into his house. Ellie said, "Do you mind waiting?"

"We're going to wait all afternoon for her to come out?" Mill hissed.

Ellie smiled, "She'll be out in under twenty minutes. I guarantee it."

"Do you have some premonition about these things granddaughter?"

"You're familiar with the term *'quickie,'* I presume."

"You seem to forget I was a flapper in the twenties going to speak easies in Manhattan. I wasn't born under a spinach leaf, you know."

"She's got to get back to the parade. She'll be acting like she's been looking all over for Michter."

"You seem to know all about this kind of behavior."

Ellie, doing an imitation of Mill said, *"You seem to forget I was a flapper..."*

Mill slugged her on the arm and said, "Okay, smart girl. That's enough out of you."

They chatted for another nineteen minutes and out of the front door came Jessica, but not before she gave a shirtless Winnington a big wet kiss goodbye.

"Well, at least we know where Winnington keeps his clothes and car."

They let Jessica get a safe distance away and then they went away from their hideout behind the forsythia. They followed Jessica back into town, and sure enough halfway down Main Street in a loud voice, they heard her say, "Where have you two been? I've been looking all over for you!" to Michter and Chambers. She slid her arm into Michter's, gave him a big kiss on the cheek, and off they went.

"That girl is playing a dangerous game," Mill said.

Ellie didn't need any extra hints of infidelity. "She's just a tramp looking for the highest bidder."

"Whoa!" Mill said. "I didn't teach you to talk like that!"

Mill watched the three of them go merrily down Main Street like Dorothy, the Scarecrow, and the Tin Man traversing the Yellow Brick Road before they came upon the Cowardly Lion.

Ellie had been put in a bad humor. "C'mon, let's go."

And they made off for home.

As they walked the half mile or so back to home, Mill said, "That was a good shot old Bill made."

Ellie, harrumphed, "If Bill shot that pistol, I'm Madonna."

"Who's Madonna?"

"Never mind."

"You don't think that was an accident?"

"Not in the slightest. And neither did Claude."

"Then what are you thinking?"

"I think it was a warning."

"A warning?"

"One of those three men needed to be warned about something."

"Wow, you jump right to conclusions, don't you."

"And when was the last time a gun went off—even a pellet gun—at the Memorial Day parade?"

"Never. But that doesn't mean there's foul play afoot."

"Save for two dead people. And another dead guy this morning."

"And a big hotel going up. Okay, maybe not a coincidence."

"My first question is, 'Who did the shooting?'"

"Unlikely Bill."

"And my second, 'Which of the three were they shooting at?'"

They discussed this for several minutes and by the time they reached Mill's house, they had pretty much convinced themselves that they were getting way ahead of themselves.

A small beat-up Honda was parked in Mill's driveway and Ellie's door was open. She sprinted up the stairs with her fists clenched, ready to do battle once again.

Getting to the top of the stairs and lunging into her room, she found a thirtyish man with premature graying hair and thick horn-rimmed black nerd glasses. He was looking at Ellie's phone that he had expertly taken apart and had spread out with precision on her drafting table. When he turned around he was holding a pair of needle-nose pliers. The pliers were holding a green disc about the size of a communion wafer with embedded diodes on it and two thin wires coming out of the disc.

The man said, not looking at her as he observed the disc as if it were a rare jungle specimen, "What makes you so interesting that someone would want to put a listening device this sophisticated into your phone?"

Ellie, trying not to completely freak out said, "I really don't know."

"Someone is very interested in knowing what you know."

"I don't know anything! I'm spending the week with my grandmother! I've been coming out here since I was born!"

He finally made eye contact with her by looking over the nerd glasses that had slid down his nose. He very certainly didn't believe her. He turned his attention back to the disc, "Okay, since you're not going to be very helpful."

"Wait," she interrupted. "Who *are* you?"

"I'm David Most, Claude's friend. He told me to find out if someone is listening in on your phone."

"I'm telling you. I don't know anything. Do I think something is going on in this town with this hotel going in, yes?"

"Are you the person trying to put the hotel in? Or block it?"

"Neither. Though the people who are putting up the hotel asked me to do their logo, that's it!"

"You're not really helping me," he said flatly.

Ellie got flustered, "Look, hotels aren't bad things. Do I think there should be one in Sounion? That's for the town to decide. Not me!"

"Let's skip over that and look at what we know," he said as he showed her the disc. "I pulled this out of the speaker part of the handset of your phone. It is the latest model and then some, so it's been put in very recently. Likely, in the past few days. Maybe even yesterday or the day before. Who have you called?"

"No one!"

"Someone was listening in on you."

Ellie took in a breath. The man was here because she told Morgan that she thought someone was listening to her. As flustered as she was with all of his questions, and frankly, judgements, he was an ally. "The only call I've placed was to my assistant over the weekend, for heaven's sake, it's Memorial Day weekend."

"No one else, no boyfriend? Call to your mom? Anything?"

"Are you trying to be ironic?"

He didn't understand the question, "What did you tell your assistant?"

"To send a messenger out here because I decided to stay here for the week."

"And what happened?"

"The real messenger was carjacked by someone, he pretended to be the real messenger and then threatened me and then tried to rape me."

True concern washed over David Most's face, "Oh," he paused. "I'm sorry, I didn't know that. I thought this was just some pervert creep listening in on you talking dirty to your boyfriend. Or you're some celebrity that I don't recognize."

"He said I was asking a lot of questions, but when I was asking all my questions, it was in a crowded restaurant with everyone I've met since coming out here."

"I'll try to do some digging and see if anyone's bought one of these in the last few days. There's only a few places in the city and Long Island where you could buy something this sophisticated, and it sure ain't cheap."

"Thank you," she said meekly.

"I've got one last question for you: Do you want me to put it back in?"

"*What?!*"

"Calm down," he said as he gestured with his hands. "I always ask because: One, do you want them to know that *you* know you've been bugged? And two, it is an excellent source of spreading *dis*information to the person who thinks they're getting prime and true information from you."

"Isn't the word 'misinformation?'"

He smiled, "In my line of work, you quickly learn the difference. Misinformation is accidentally giving inaccurate information. Disinformation is giving inaccurate information—or true information you want them to hear that they shouldn't hear—intentionally."

A hint of an impish grin emerged across Ellie's face, "Why, David Most, you scoundrel." Her grin grew to a beaming smile as she looked at her phone. She looked over at him, "Darn right you're going to put that bugger back in there."

And David Most made it so.

Chapter 17.

Sleuthing in the dunes

For the rest of the day, Ellie did more work for her firm drafting correspondence, working on estimates for new clients, and refining sketches for Roger Michter.

A frustration and a curiosity was growing in her that was manifesting into action. She wanted to know what was going on with all these hotel people. They show up and dead people show up along with them? Her impulse was to call Claude Morgan and say, "Do something!" But she'd asked that the bug be put back in.

They're hotel people and they want to build a hotel. That's what they do. Why not in Sounion? There are no hotels here. The closest one is a twenty-minute drive. And maybe downtown is getting a little run down and not every third storefront needed to be a real estate office.

Ellie got to where she was by action. All of the roadblocks in her career, she'd mostly hurdled. Yes, she'd fallen a time or two, but she always got up like a baseball closer who gives up a game-winning grand slam one night and the next night pitches like the king of the sport.

As the Sun was about to go below the horizon, she got up and put on black jeans, her black Chuck Taylors and a hooded black sweatshirt. Her first foray into a little sleuthing brought the news that Jessica was two-timing with James Winnington III. She thought she'd hoof the two miles across the beach and dunes to Roger Michter's place and maybe listen in to get some information.

For stress reduction and fitness, Ellie ran three miles every morning. Rain, sleet, freezing temperatures, she would smile and wave to the early morning post office folks and newspaper deliverers near her home in the city as she got her mileage in.

Ellie didn't make quick work of the two miles over to Roger Michter's because running across the beach and dunes after the sun had set wasn't easy. About halfway there, she unceremoniously tripped over a clump of beach grass near a sand fence and went ass over tea kettle into the sand getting some into her mouth.

"Oh, Ellie Pincrest, you suave spy!" she poked at herself.

She got up and made her way near Roger Michter's isolated house and positioned herself behind a steep inclined dune about ten yards from the side of the house. She could see the driveway, the entire side of the house with all the windows open, and the sprawling back deck.

And what did she come upon? A typical early summer weekday evening in Sounion. Jessica was watching an episode of *Who's the Boss* and munching on some popcorn while lounging on an oversized sofa and ottoman. She had the sound turned up, the live studio audience punctuating Ellie's inability to hear anything inside.

Roger Michter was at the kitchen table with several spreadsheets eating an apple. Workaholic.

It stayed like that for seemingly forever. The wind began to pick up and grains of sand began to get into Ellie's hair, eyes, ears, mouth, and clothes.

A silver Porsche 911 pulled into the driveway blaring Frank Sinatra on the car's enormous Blaupunkt stereo and subwoofer. Out of the car came Morris Barkwell, the attorney for the hotel. He had on tennis whites and was still a little sweaty. He'd must've played until the sun went down. He had a sweatband on his right wrist.

He pulled his worn leather briefcase out of the passenger's side and walked up to the front door, knocked and was warmly greeted by Roger Michter. Ellie could hear them small talking about this and that when James Winnington drove up, got out and went inside. The three of them talked some more, clearly waiting for someone as they looked at their watches.

Mayor Archie Richardson drove up in his seemingly century-old Toyota Land Cruiser. Richardson did not immediately get out of the car. In the driveway, he stared straight ahead. The wind was really beginning to pick up. No rain was in sight, it was just a typical windswept night on the southern shore of Long Island.

After a couple of silent minutes sitting in his Land Cruiser, Richardson slowly got out, but as he did so he looked around several times to make sure no one saw him at this house. He wore an oversized Hawaiian shirt, cargo shorts, and Birkenstocks. As he went up the steps of the house, Roger Michter appeared at the front door with a big smile on his face. He put his thumb and index finger in the position of a gun and made *bang-bang* sounds.

Richardson found this funny not in the slightest and said, "Shove it, Michter. That was no accident. You think you can pressure me?"

Michter said, "Oh, come on. What are you talking about? They found the guy and he said it was an accident. A harmless accident. We don't need pressure. We're here to help this community!"

"You call this 'harmless?'" he yelled as he pointed to his shoulder that had been winged earlier in the day. "And wasn't it a coincidence one of your people made a citizen's arrest." It wasn't a question.

Now it was Michter's turn to look around to make sure no one heard. "Oh, Archie. You're fine. Everything's fine. Don't be so dramatic."

"Speaking of, where is the great Beckwith Chambers, anyway?"

"He won't be here tonight. Other business."

"Really? He makes a big thing of coming here and then he doesn't come to your big pre-vote meeting?"

"He's a very busy man."

"Undoubtedly, but you'd think he'd be here for a strategy meeting."

"How is the town council going to vote?" Michter asked.

"It's split. In the case of a tie, I'm the tiebreaker. Which is why I'm guessing I got," he paused for effect. "Shot in the arm today."

"Oh, what an imagination! You know I was doing a big hotel on Martha's Vineyard several years ago, and a state senator up there was convinced I was poisoning him. Ha! He's a congressman now, so maybe I was his good luck charm!"

Michter kept laughing and Richardson kept frowning as they went into the house.

Jessica put down her popcorn, poured glasses of white wine for Michter, Winnington, Barkwell, Richardson, and herself.

They looked over maps and spreadsheets for several minutes, but as the wind picked up Ellie could hear less and less. The only scraps of words and sentences she got were:

"Wine," from Jessica.

"Pressure," from Richardson pointing at Michter.

"Recourse," from Barkwell who smiled like a tennis-clad snake and pointed to his briefcase.

"Target," from Winnington as he spread his arms wide.

"Majority," from Michter with a satisfying grin.

But when Michter said that, Richardson flew into a rage and Ellie could very clearly hear, "I'm out. You've got to be kidding me. Go somewhere else with your hotel!"

He spun around and made for the door. Michter, Winnington, Barkwell, Richardson all tried to get in his way but he shrugged everyone off and ripped open the door and yelled again, "I'm out!"

In his rush, he stumbled over a something on the dark walkway going to the driveway, but didn't fall. As he opened his car door, the front door of the house opened. Richardson turned the ignition in the Land Cruiser and it just made a *wuh-wuh* sound and didn't turn over. Someone was walking down the walkway but Ellie couldn't see who it was immediately.

The person who walked up to the side of Richardson's Land Cruiser was Jessica Traverts, asking Richardson to roll down his window. She was hopping up and down like an anxious cheerleader whose team is on the two-yard line with time running out.

"I'm out! Voting no!" she heard him yell from inside the Land Cruiser.

"Please?" she asked. More cheerleader hopping.

Reluctantly, the window came down. Ellie couldn't hear what she said, but whatever the heck it was, Richardson got out of Land Cruiser, slammed the door shut and went back inside. Maybe it was the hopping because she kept it up all the way back inside the door.

The group met for another hour, and things got testy to say the least, but everything was certainly in a low growl instead of the yelling before. Ellie couldn't hear anything, but they were plying him with wine and margaritas the rest of the meeting.

The meeting broke up and they all went on their separate ways. Winnington, surprisingly adroit under the hood, even helped Richardson get the Land Cruiser started.

Ellie jogged back to her place. When she got there, the phone was ringing. It was well after ten.

"Hello."

"Ellie? Ellie Pincrest?" a man with an airy British voice said.

"Yes. Who's this?"

"Oh, Ellie. I'm offended. I was hoping you'd remember me. It's Sir Reginald Twekes. You did the logo for my British aerospace company about five years ago."

Pulling herself together, Ellie hurriedly said, "Sir Reggie. Wow! I'm so sorry, I just, uh, wasn't expecting a call from you."

He giggled, "Well, young lady, your assistant told me—do you know your assistant works on Memorial Day?"

"That sounds like him. I didn't ask him to."

"I was just leaving a message for you at the office when he picked up the office phone. He said he was reorganizing all the color swatches in the office."

"That also sounds like him."

Another giggle. "He told me that is was a 'sign of weakness' to not work on a holiday."

"Again, sounds like him."

Another giggle. "He said that you were spending the week after Memorial Day out at your grandmother's in a place called Sounion Cove on Long Island."

"I am."

"Well, I'm asking for an imposition."

"Sure, anything Sir Reggie." Reginald Twekes had long ago been knighted by the Queen for his many contributions to her majesty's fighter jets.

We are buying an up and coming aerospace firm located not far from your offices in Manhattan. They need a logo now that they're hitting the big time with us. The missus and I are in Manhattan for only one more day before we hop back over the pond again, and I'm wondering—and I greatly apologize—could you come into the city for a meeting tomorrow to discuss the logo? I really must insist that I'm in on the meeting. The president of the firm we're buying from is a former academic and my fear is that he'll ask you to make a logo featuring a slide rule."

Ellie smiled. She'd been in dozens of meetings where the smartest person in the room also thought they were smart enough to design the logo. It was not a recipe for success.

"I'll be there. What time?"

"Eleven. Okay by you? Park and Fifty-seventh. That big glass building. Eleventh floor."

"I know it. I have a couple other clients in that building. I'll take the seaplane back in the morning."

"Splendid. Don't skimp on your fees with him. This guy is going to be loaded beyond his wildest dreams for the rest of his life."

"Oh, I won't. Goodbye, Sir Reggie."

And she rung off.

She pulled out the well-worn card of Mac the Pilot to make a reservation on the seaplane. There were several executives that had weekend homes in Sounion and the day after Memorial Day might be booked up with them going back into the city after a long weekend with the family in Sounion.

Her goal was simply to leave a message and beg. If she didn't get on the seaplane that meant either Mill had to drive her into the city or take the train for two hours.

On the first ring, Mac the Pilot answered. Ellie wasn't expecting him to answer so she stammered for a moment.

In a gruff voice, Mac the Pilot said, "If this is some phone sex call, you picked the absolutely wrong person."

"Mac, uh. It's me. Ellie Pincrest. I thought I would be getting your answering machine."

"Phone's near my bed."

"Oh, wonderful. Uh, I've got a surprise meeting in the city. Do you think I could hop a ride tomorrow into the city?"

"Are you planning to sit with the luggage in the back compartment?"

"Uh, no. Was hoping I could sit up with you and your passengers."

After a pause, he said, "You're in luck. I've got a cancellation. But, I can't take you back in the afternoon. I'm on other runs tomorrow."

"That's fine. I'll stay in my apartment in Manhattan."

"We're scheduled to take-off at eight in the morning, but could you be there about fifteen minutes early?

"Certainly. See you then."

Chapter 18.

You can't partially exist

Ellie was at the dock right at 7:45. Two smartly-dressed executive types were already getting on the plane. Mac the Pilot was there and he motioned for her to quickly get on.

She did and he fired up the engine. He taxied the plane away from the dock. Ellie noticed another smartly-dressed executive type get out of the passenger-side of a gray Volvo station wagon and start running down the dock waving his arms while trying not to hit himself in the head with his briefcase.

"Hey, there's Pete," one of the executive types in the back seat said.

Yawning, the executive type next to him said, "Isn't he supposed to be on this plane into the city? He usually is this time of the morning."

Mac the Pilot said, "No, no. Of course not. He didn't make a reservation."

Ellie looked over to Mac the Pilot and he winked at her. Although it was morning, he handed over his signature large bag of candy and a Pepsi.

The flight into Manhattan was uneventful and they landed without a bump. Ellie sometimes got a little nervous about flying and often upon landing, she would whisper to herself, "Cheated death, again."

She made her way up to Park and Fifty-seventh. Sir Reggie met her there and the meeting went better than she expected. With the prospect of nearly eternal riches, the aerospace geek would've taken a drawing of a single straight black line as his logo.

After the meeting, Sir Reggie and Ellie walked down the street. He was off to meet his wife and an old friend before taking the Concorde back to London. She was headed to her office so they had about three blocks together to chat.

Ellie started, "I'm working on a hotel logo for someone you probably know. Beckwith Chambers. He's British."

Sir Reggie laughed, "My, dear. Just because I am knighted does not give me acquaintance with every person in the British Isles."

"No, I mean. He's British and, uh, well, rich."

Sir Reggie laughed again and in the exact same voice said, "My, dear. Just because I am knighted—"

Ellie cut him off and said, "I know. I know. What I mean is he's very rich."

"You mean 'very rich' like me?"

"Not to put too fine a point on it, but yes."

"What's this bloke's name again?"

"Beckwith Chambers."

Without hesitation, Sir Reggie said, "Never heard of him."

"Really?"

"Never in all my life."

"Don't all of you?"

"All of you, what? Do you think we have the 'Very Rich Person's' club and we sit around and talk about being rich?"

"No, I mean that in your business dealings, you'd run into one another."

"That's true, but I'm sorry. I've never heard of him. Would you like one of my assistants to find out about him?"

"No, I don't think so."

They came to the corner where their paths would diverge and Sir Reggie kissed Ellie's hand and bid her a fond farewell and said he looked forward to seeing her again the next time he was in Manhattan.

Ellie walked over to her office not far from Park and Fifty-seventh. Bobby, her assistant greeted her with a big smile and handed her a large caramel-color coffee from the office kitchen. Because the messenger company had called the office earlier that morning profusely apologizing for the attack that happened both to their messenger and to Ellie, the entire office knew how close the boss came to not being with them anymore. As this happened so soon after her ex's betrayal, they were overwhelmed with concern for her. *En masse*, they left their desks and drafting tables and gave hugs, little gifts.

Ellie didn't have an office. She didn't like doors in the slightest. When she was named President, it was the first thing she had the building do: Remove the doors of senior staffers to make sure the office was more open, more accessible. Ellie's "office" was actually in the middle of the open office in the "bullpen" as they called it in a small sea of drafting tables. As a matter of fact, the only things that had doors in the office were the men's room and the ladies' rooms. Someone had once joked in a staff meeting, "So, Boss. When are those coming off?"

She told Bobby that today was going to be the only day she would be in the office this week. Over the course of the next few hours, she and her staff went over several projects, including the Sounion Hotel project. For the Sounion project, there were several logos already done and presented, some great, some not so. The "not so great" designs were eliminated. There were a lot of comments on the logos they would keep with "vibrant" or "vivid" or "brilliant" or "needs refining" associated with them. In the past couple of years, the firm had bought a fleet of the new Apple Macintoshes to assist with logo development. The office was split about sixty-forty. Sixty percent loved this new Macintosh and forty percent said, "Using a computer to design art, is not designing art."

As the meeting was wrapping up, the phone rang and Bobby picked it up, as always, on the first ring. He listened for a moment, nodded his head and put the caller on hold. He looked at Ellie and said, "It's an Officer Morgan from the Sounion police department; he'd like to speak with you."

The meeting broke up and everyone went back to their work stations. Ellie picked up her phone and said, "How did you find me?"

"Mill."

"Not sure why I even asked."

"I'm back from a meeting with the coroner about the second kid, the one with the skewed hat that appeared to be a drug overdose. *Skewed Hat* did not die from a drug overdose. He died, like *Ripped Jeans*, of drowning, and he'd been moved. He had cocaine in him, but he didn't die of it and it doesn't seem the cocaine made him pass out and drown."

Ellie was a little too stunned to speak immediately, then asked, "How can someone drown and then show up in a park in the middle of Sounion with a drug needle in their arm?"

"Coroner said he'd been knocked unconscious and drowned. Almost like he was knocked unconscious while he was swimming. He also had similar trauma to his chest that Ripped Jeans had to his hip. Like a whale hit him in the chest with his tail. And he swam himself to death."

"Wouldn't a whale tail kind of break them in half? Also, don't drowning victims wash ashore?"

"Whatever happened to this kid, he'd been fished out of the drink and stuck in the park. Maybe he got run over by a car, put in the drink unconscious, then taken to the park and stuck with needles. I've got a half-dozen viable scenarios written out. Someone went out of their way to show him with his skewed hat to humiliate him further in death. We didn't know he'd drown because it had rained overnight the night we found him. And, of course, someone stuck a cocaine needle in his arm in the hope of misleading the coroner."

"Well, I was going to tell you when I got back tomorrow, but I did some sleuthing yesterday regarding the hotel people."

There was silence and Morgan said ruefully, "You want to run that by me again? It sounded like you said you were 'doing some sleuthing yesterday,' but I seem to remember from somewhere that you design logos for a living."

"After the parade yesterday and that whole thing with Mayor Richardson getting winged in the arm, I followed James Winnington III to his rental home in town. It was bugging me that I didn't know where he lived or his relationship with the hotel people. Remember, he doesn't work for Michter, he's the investment banker that matches the money with the deal."

"So he's the guy who brought in that British guy Beckwith Chambers?"

"I think so, but there was a meeting last night at Michter's house that Chambers wasn't at."

"Wait, I thought you went to Winnington's house."

"I did in the afternoon."

"Then when did you go to Michter's house and why would they invite you to a meeting?"

"Actually, I wasn't invited."

"And you just showed up and said, 'I'm here for your meeting?'"

"I was hiding out behind a sand dune near Michter's house. It was later in the evening."

"Back up, back up. When you followed Winnington home after the parade, where were you?"

"Across the street behind a forsythia."

"And you did this alone?"

"Mill was with me at Winnington's because we went right after the parade."

"Should I even ask what you've found out?"

"Not as much as I'd like. First, Winnington is having an affair with the caterer, Jessica Traverts."

"The girlfriend of Roger Michter."

"Yes."

"And you think this is helping to find out what happened to two dead people? Because that's what I really care about."

"I'm just telling you I observed maybe a fracture in the hotel people."

"Does Michter know?"

"No. Unless he's incredibly open minded."

"That girl better be careful, the way things have played out the last few days, and she could end up dead."

"It crossed my mind."

"And what did you find out at Michter's house? How did you get there? Isn't that a couple of miles from Mill's place? And didn't you imply the meeting was at night? Can you even drive?"

"I ran down the beach, cut through some of the beachfront properties, and over the dunes."

"You're unbelievable." It wasn't a compliment.

"I didn't find out as much as I wanted there either. The meeting participants were Michter, of course, with Jessica as they live together."

"For now, it seems."

"Mayor Richardson was there along with Morris Barkwell, the lawyer, and Winnington."

"What happened?"

"Unfortunately, I had trouble hearing because of all that wind last night, but I clearly heard these words: *Wine, Bait, Recourse, Target,* and *Majority*."

"And those words are going to help me find out what's going on?"

"I don't know. But, the interesting thing that did happen was Archie Richardson abruptly started yelling 'I'm out!' over and over, then stormed out of the meeting."

"And where did he go after he stormed out?"

"Jessica Traverts convinced him to go back in. She must be the person who tries to smooth things out for her boyfriend."

"Whichever boyfriend."

"What have you found out?" she asked.

"First, town council moved up the vote on the hotel to *tonight*."

"Can they do that?"

"They just did. I think Mayor Richardson wants this over one way or another. Which makes your description of his reaction at the meeting rather germane."

"How is the vote going to go?"

"Don't know. Has Mill said anything to you about it?"

"No, but I'll find out."

"I'll find out some more on my side. Maybe you should stand down on this investigating."

"Someone attacked me. I'm taking it somewhat personally."

They rung off and Ellie called Bobby over, "Could you do a favor for me?"

"Anything, Boss," he said as if he were a horse in the starting gate at Pimlico.

"Go down to the New York Public Library and find out all you can on a guy named 'Beckwith Chambers.' British. Billionaire. Reclusive."

"What are we looking for?"

"If he exists."

Bobby raised his eyebrows and said, "Oh that is *so* cool! On it, Boss. Back in a couple of hours." He pretty much ran through the front door of the office because opening it would've taken too much time.

Meetings on several projects went on throughout the morning. A short time after lunch, Bobby, breathless, appeared with a file folder of Xeroxed sheets, he held them aloft like Perseus holding the head of Medusa.

Ellie followed Bobby into the big glass conference room and he began laying sheets out in a pre-arranged order.

"Does he exist?" she asked.

"That depends."

"I really don't like that answer, Bobby."

"Let me break it down for you. He exists in the media, but nowhere else."

"Explain."

"I found a couple two or three dozen articles about him doing charity work over the past few years, but there is nothing in the *Wall Street Journal* or *New York Times* about him in business. Any mention of him is charity-related. He was on Page Six in the *New York Post* a few times, the latest was at a gallery opening. The caption is 'British Billionaire looks to add to his art collection.'"

"So what's the problem? He exists, right?"

"It depends," he regretted it as soon as it came out of his mouth.

"Bobby, not in the mood for word games."

"Boss, I've broken the articles out by year," he said as he pointed to the five short stacks of Xeroxed sheets.

"But?"

"But, he doesn't exist before five years ago. Was he born a billionaire? People like him are featured and interviewed in *Fortune* on their way up with their businesses. They have a product they sell and it's in the *Wall Street Journal*. Et cetera, Et cetera. This guy just showed up in London and New York City as 'British Billionaire.'"

"Maybe he inherited the money."

"People like that already *have* money before they inherit a billion dollars. That's just their big payday, if he comes from money, he's spending family money way before."

"Well, I've seen him in the flesh." Ellie said with some resignation.

Bobby pulled out an item from "Page Six" of the *New York Post*, the gossip and society page of New York. It says here, "British billionaire donates large check to inner city reading program." There was a photo with a smiling Beckwith Chambers with a city council member and leggy Hollywood starlets.

"He's got money."

"That he does."

"He funds the real estate deals that Roger Michter does, like the one we're working on in Sounion."

Ellie could feel frustration rising in her, but she didn't know why. What was the big deal about Beckwith Chambers and why did she have to know if he was real or not? Worse, why could she not let it go?

The intercom chirping in the conference room made her jump. Bobby pounced on it. He listened a moment, stiffened, and said, "Sir Reginald Twekes for you."

"I thought you'd be on your supersonic plane by now," Ellie said.

"My darling wife and I are boarding now. I'm calling from a payphone next to the Concorde gate. Look, I know you told me not to look up this Beckwith Chambers, but you know how I am about doing what someone tells me not to do."

"Could be your middle name Sir Reggie."

He giggled in the way only the British do. "Anyway, I have certain people who work in official places that will do certain favors for me and I asked them to look for this Beckwith Chambers. It intrigued me also that I didn't know him. I guess it was a certain mark against my vanity if you will."

"And what did they say?"

"Is he about 50 or so?"

"Yes."

"Sandy hair?"

"Yes."

"He exists."

"So they tell me."

"What does that mean?"

"Never mind. What did your people say?"

He made a clucking sound with his tongue, like he was studying his notes. "He's got a tax ID number. He's registered with National Health. He's been in the Fleet Street gossip columns. A lot of press releases."

"But."

"I can't say it any other way: *Why don't I know him?* Seriously, there aren't that many of us in England after they taxed us blind here in the seventies."

"Did he make his money in Monaco or Switzerland? He's just born in England?"

"Maybe."

"Did your people say what he does?"

"They said 'inheritance.'"

"Sounds like you're about to say, "But."

"Who did he inherit it from? There's no billionaire 'Chambers' anywhere. That I would most certainly know."

"Interesting."

"Look, they're closing the door on the plane and my wife is stomping her foot. Ta-ta, darling. I'll speak to you if I find out anything more."

"Thank you, Sir Reggie. You didn't need to go to this much trouble."

"My logo is everywhere from Southampton to Aberdeen, and I have you to thank for that."

"You're very welcome, Sir Reggie. Safe flight, sir."

And he rung off.

"More mystery concerning Mr. Beckwith Chambers?" asked Bobby.

Ellie stared out the window. "He seems to only partially exist."

"That's what I've been trying to tell you, Boss! You can't partially exist!"

Chapter 19.

Pink sand

Late in the day, Ellie and her team put together all the logos they would be showing Roger Michter. She put them into her portfolio case and went back to her apartment.

She said hello to her doorman who commented that he hadn't seen her in several days and Ellie remembered it was the first time she'd seen him since she found out that Stephen had gone off and gotten married.

Opening the door to her apartment, she felt an abject loneliness she hadn't felt since the initial gut punch last Friday when she heard the news. She seemed to remember all the times that Stephen had stayed overnight over the years. All the times they'd ordered in Chinese on Sunday nights. All the times he'd waited patiently at her door fidgeting while she found a scarf or whatnot before they caught a Broadway show. He'd bought her a Warhol signed print of Elizabeth Taylor, Ellie's favorite actress, a few years back, and it took center stage in one's line of site when you walked through the door. Her first thought tonight as she walked through was to throw it out the window. She vetoed the idea. Though Andy Warhol's star had significantly faded by the year 1986, she had a feeling it would be worth a great deal of money someday. And, she just loved it—Liz too.

She worried that she'd have trouble getting to sleep or staying asleep because of the rough waters that Stephen had provided her. Instead, she slept like she'd run back-to-back marathons.

The next morning was bright and sunny and she was glad the flying back out to Sounion would be smooth. She did her usual three mile morning run, showered, and got dressed to make it down to the seaplane dock.

Mac the Pilot was waiting for her. He looked like he'd died, been brought back to life, died again, and brought half back to life. The dark circles under his eyes looked as if they'd been magic-markered in. He'd not shaved, and by the smell of his breath, hadn't even bothered with a Tic-Tac.

When he spoke, he sounded like he'd been gargling with Drano since yesterday. "You're late," he croaked.

"I'm twenty minutes early."

He looked at his watch, then moved it closer to and away from his face, squinting his eyes. He spoke briefly about Jesus, Mary, and Joseph, and then looked at her with bloodshot eyes and said, "I stand corrected."

"Am I the only one?"

"I'm doing mostly shipping today."

"What are you shipping?"

"Look." He opened the passenger door and there were six cases of wine smartly seat-belted and roped in. He opened the small storage cubby hole and there were two more wine cases.

"Wow. Who's throwing a party?"

"It's for that caterer, Jessica Traverts. Michter's girlfriend. Some big shindig. She asked for a favor to bring out this wine. One of the big wine wholesalers in Manhattan dropped it off a while ago. I'm doing this at cost for her which I'm guessing only an idiot would do. Go ahead and get in. If you notice that I can't wedge myself in, it's because my head feels like it's the size the Goodyear blimp."

"Why so tired?"

"Just running around."

As Mac the Pilot taxied out to take off from the East River, Ellie looked down at the floor boards and noticed pink sand all over the place.

"Where's the pink sand from?"

"Some new hot Ivy League bar in Manhattan has pink sand on the floor instead of saw dust. I took out some people very early this morning. Practically sunrise. They'd never gone to sleep. Got sand everywhere and you can't just fly into a car wash and vacuum it out."

It was a smooth trip back. She didn't even do her usual *Cheated death* thought when they landed.

It was another hot, steamy day. As Ellie looked over at the dock in Sounion, she saw Jessica waiting for the plane.

Mac the Pilot cut the engine and the lines were secured. Jessica said as Mac the Pilot opened the door, "I really appreciate you doing this!" She gave him a little peck on the cheek and he gave her a big smile. The cynical side of Ellie asked if she was involved with Mac the Pilot as well.

"Don't mention it. No trouble at all."

"Can you bill me? I'll put it on the invoice for the party."

"I'll have it to you later today."

"Thanks," she said as she started hoisting cases out.

"Can I help?" asked Ellie.

"Absolutely. Thank you," said Jessica in a strained voice as she lifted out a case awkwardly from the back seat.

Mac the Pilot joined in as James Winnington drove up in his car. "Ladies," he paused. "And gentleman. I'm here to offer lifting and transporting assistance. Roger has a meeting with the Mayor regarding tonight's vote and couldn't be here."

Winnington and Jessica stole a glance at each other that they didn't think anyone saw, but Jessica caught. They got everything into Winnington's car. They even tied two cases to the suitcase rack on the back.

"Can we give you a ride home?" Winnington asked.

She shook her head, "No."

As they were tying down the last case, Ellie noticed something on the front of Mac the Pilot's airplane: grime. And lots of it. She pointed to it and said, "In addition to that pink sand, you'll need to remove all that grime to keep your seaplane looking ship shape."

Mac the Pilot walked around to the grimy cowling and said, "True, I've been doing a lot of trips back and forth to Manhattan. I'll take her up in the next severe thunderstorm and get her super soaked."

Ellie waved goodbye to Mac the Pilot and the Jessica-Winnington combo drove off in his car. They turned and likely off to his rented house for a rendezvous, and not straight through the light and off to Roger Michter's beach house.

Ellie murmured, "None of my business." But, as she walked up toward the light herself, she added, "Maybe."

When she got back to Mill's place, she was doing some weed cutting along her white sea shell driveway. Most of the homes in Sounion had recycled sea shells, instead of gravel, for driveways. The sun bleaches the shell's color to white.

"Nice day yesterday in Manhattan?"

"A little confounding. This Beckwith Chambers fellow is a real mystery."

"And why are you so concerned with Mr. Beckwith Chambers?"

"I don't know. Who is he? Where does he come from? He's *just* a 'British Billionaire' who obviously exists and is in the press. Heck, he's even on Page Six of the *Post.*"

"So?"

"And, they had a big meeting over at Roger Michter's and he didn't even show up. If you're pumping in that kind of money to start a hotel, you'd think he'd be there."

"Were you at this meeting?"

She didn't speak because she knew Mill had sprung a trap and then reluctantly said, "Kind of."

"Granddaughter, would you mind telling me what that means?"

"I wanted to do a little sleuthing so I dressed in all black and hid behind a sand dune and listened to them."

There was a very long silence from Mill. Even after Ellie said a pleading, "Say something!"

Mill finally said, "And what do you suspect?"

"That's what I don't know. Everything seems legitimate, but who are these people? And why do bad things happen when they get here?"

"The vote is tonight, a council member can't vote no on the circumstantial. We're talking about a lot of jobs."

Ellie asked, "Are there *any* pink sand beaches on Long Island?"

"That's not the question I thought you were going to ask after I said what I said."

"I know, but it might be important."

"You know there's no pink sand beaches here."

"Why?"

"Because pink sand is caused by foraminifera, a little microscopic organism that's got a red shell. It mixes with coral, and there's no coral anywhere near Long Island, and certainly not near Sounion. Why do you ask?"

"Mac the Pilot."

"What about him?"

"I just flew out in his seaplane. There was pink sand all over the floor boards."

"So?"

"You just said there's no pink sand anywhere. He said there's a new bar in Manhattan that has pink sand instead of saw dust on the floors."

"Even I know that bar story is a lie."

They said in almost perfect unison, "Mac the Pilot doesn't think like a woman."

"A woman in high heels wouldn't go anywhere near a bar with a thin layer of sand on a hardwood floor. She'd slip and fall within seconds," Mill said.

"Why did he lie to me?"

"Because he doesn't want you to know where he's been."

"Where's he been?"

"Somewhere pink."

"I also noticed the cowling on the plane was really grimy, like he'd been on a long trip. He told me that I'd have to stay in the city yesterday and not come back last night because he had other trips to make. And, he looked like death warmed over this morning."

"I can see the wheels spinning in your head."

"Where are there pink sand beaches near Long Island? Nowhere on the eastern seaboard, right?"

"Three places," Mill said as she pulled some weeds near the driveway. "Horseshoe Bay and Elbow Beach in Bermuda. Your grandfather and I would go there often for weekend getaways. The second is Pink Sands Beach near Miami, and the last is several beaches in The Bahamas."

"Sounds like The Bermuda Triangle."

"Not really. Horseshoe and Elbow are the two most popular beaches in Bermuda, you just can't drop your airplane out of the sky and pull up to a beach. You're going to make a scene and they really do appreciate it when you land at or near the airport with a flight plan."

"What other beach besides Bermuda doesn't fit?"

"Miami. That's only about three miles of shoreline, and again, you can't just land your plane in Miami and pull up on the beach. A Miami police car is going to come over and ask what the heck you think you're doing."

"So that leaves The Bahamas."

"Which is made up of a lot of separate isolated islands—with pink sand beaches."

"I didn't ask him if he picked up anyone in The Bahamas."

"He wouldn't have taken Beckwith Chambers down there would he?"

"No, Chambers would fly in a Lear Jet, right? It's too far for a billionaire in a little seaplane, but, a seaplane could get there and back in less than a day. Maybe someone who doesn't want to know he's gone somewhere."

Claude Morgan drove up in his squad car.

"We were just talking about you, after a fashion," Mill said.

"More sleuthing?" he said to Mill but was looking at Ellie.

Ellie crossed her arms self-consciously and said, "Things aren't adding up."

"You look tired," Mill said to Claude.

"Sure. There was a break-in at the pharmacy. Looks like juveniles. Just tore the place up. Can't really tell if anything was stolen besides what juveniles would find interesting. Looks like they were in a hurry and maybe done right after closing the night before. Only about two minute's worth of trashing." He looked at them and asked, "What's not adding up."

"Flying back this morning there was pink sand on the floorboards of Mac's seaplane."

"So?"

Mill asked, "Where is there pink sand?"

"Everywhere but Sounion, right?"

"Spoken like a true Canadian. You think everything is south and warm," Mill laughed.

"Mill tells me only Bermuda, Miami, and The Bahamas—and we've eliminated Bermuda and Miami."

He looked thoughtfully for several moments, and said, "Wow." And then he looked out to the ocean.

"What does 'Wow' mean? Or are you being sarcastic?" Ellie asked.

"The bodies of the two dead young men, *Ripped Jeans* and *Skewed Hat* as you've nicknamed them, were claimed this morning. That's what I was doing after looking at more clues of the pharmacy break-in. They were cousins. An uncle took custody of both. He said they were both in and out of juvenile detention most of their lives. He told me that they had both been to The Bahamas and they were running up huge debt on their credit cards. When the uncle asked them how they could afford it, they said they'd figured a way to hit the big time and they would be big bosses making big money in the very near future. They said they'd cracked the code."

"Mac the Pilot must've flown them down there and they charged everything including the flight there."

"Seems as if I'll be asking Mac the Pilot some questions and looking at his flight log this afternoon when he gets back from his afternoon sortie into the city."

Chapter 20.

The presentation of logos

Ellie's phone rang getting near lunchtime. It was Roger Michter returning a phone call that Ellie had made asking to show the logo options.

"Wonderful, wonderful. I'm going to grab some lunch at the diner in town in about a half hour, would you care to join me? I'm excited to see them."

She agreed and a half hour later, walked into the diner. He was already there, alone, drinking a large iced tea. "Big vote tonight," he said as he looked over the well-worn menu.

"Do you think it will pass? What happens if it doesn't pass? Do you pack up and leave? Do you resubmit a plan?"

He sipped his iced tea and calmly shook his head, "We won't lose. They'd be crazy to block us."

"Yes, but—"

"No," he interrupted sharply. He caught himself and attempted some small talk, "I've been meaning to ask you, the name of your design firm is *Dedalus*, where does that come from?"

Ellie smiled, "The man I took over from, his favorite book was *Portrait of the Artist as a Young Man* by James Joyce. The main character is Stephen Dedalus. He's based on a character in Greek Mythology, *Daedulus,* who defied the status quo and was the consummate craftsman."

Michter seemed pleased that the answer took his mind off the vote. He said, "Defying the status quo, like naming a woman the new president of one of the top design firms in New York City."

They ordered and after the waitress went away, Michter asked, "May I seem them, now?"

"I think you'll like what you see." At Ellie's firm, there rarely was agreement on which logo was best or if the group of logos that was to be shown was the best group to show. One of the things Ellie loved about design and about the firm were the debates on the pros and cons of a certain logo or a group of logos. The give and take, the refinements. Putting a finer-grit sandpaper to what you were doing. The restlessness of covering all the angles that kept you up until three in the morning to make sure the designs were just right.

The logos for *Sounion-by-the-Sea*, as Michter's group called it, were an exception at Dedalus Design. Everyone agreed that these were the sharpest logos they'd done this year and that anyone reviewing them would have quite a difficult time picking their favorite. There was a breadth to them that covered every intelligent direction to take the logos. Actual applause broke out in the conference room after all the logos were agreed upon.

She handed them to Michter as he put on some reading half-glasses and she started to explain the first of the eight that they had done. She thought for a moment about how much things had changed in design over the years. Her former boss said when he presented logos in the 1960s, "I brought two things to the meeting: The design of the logo they should have, and the invoice for the project."

As Ellie was wrapping up talking about the first design and on to the second, Michter simply raised his hand, looked over his reading half-glasses and said, "I'd prefer to review these without outside commentary."

Ellie raised her eyebrows. No one had ever said that before as clients liked to get into the thinking of the designer. He looked at the first.

Then the second a little too quickly.

Then the third even faster.

The fourth, fifth, sixth, seventh, and eighth as if were dealing cards.

He stacked them up, and all of a sudden he tossed them up into the air and they fell all over the table as Ellie sat there absolutely gobsmacked.

He took off his reading glasses and matter-of-factly said, "I hate them."

"What?"

"All of them. They're terrible."

Now, Ellie Pincrest, head of Dedalus Design in New York City, had four weak spots: her mother, her ex, crying uncontrollably every time she watched *An Affair to Remember* with Cary Grant and Deborah Kerr, and *anyone* that didn't robustly appreciate and love the hard work and design that had been done on one of their logo projects. Several years ago, before she became president of the firm, she was in a presentation with a big Hollywood studio boss and he obliquely said that one of the designs—mind you, this was *after* he had picked the winning design and it didn't matter about the others—that one of the designs "looked like a phallic symbol." Ellie, not really caring if she seemed impertinent to Mr. Hollywood Bigshot, asked him if he "saw phallic symbols everywhere," and she received a sharp kick in the shin from her boss who reminded her that the winning design had already been chosen and extra commentary was, at best, superfluous.

Here in the diner, in a decibel level and tone that she didn't give a hoot about, Ellie said to Roger Michter, "Could you repeat that please? And, maybe enlighten me on what *you* found wanting in all *eight* designs that my design firm has done for you that any other hotel would snap up in a second?"

He simply shrugged his shoulders and said, "You'll have to go back to the drawing board." He laughed at the pun intended and continued, "They're not sophisticated enough for what we see for Sounion."

"Not *sophisticated* enough?" Ellie reached across the table, picked up his reading glasses, looked through them feigning hyperopia and said, "Do these things even *work*?"

"Ms. Pincrest," he said balefully, "I know that you are one of, if not the leading logo designer in New York City, I am just saying, for this project, these do not work for us. And, Ms. Pincrest, you *don't* need to be insulting."

"And you *don't* have to be a blind moron," Ellie said, smashing every rule in presentation etiquette.

Two things happened simultaneously, the food arrived, which was promising to make this one of the most awkward lunches in the history of the diner on Main Street in Sounion. The other was Mill arrived after doing some light shopping in town.

Mill walked over, gave her granddaughter a kiss on the cheek, and asked, "What a surprise! Mind if I join you?" Mill waved over to the waitress, smiled, and asked for an iced tea with lemon.

Mill immediately picked up on the tension in the booth. "So, is something the matter with you two?"

Ellie replied sardonically, "Mr. Michter's reading glasses are malfunctioning."

"Stop it!" he said.

Mill reached over and took the logo designs from the table and went through them, "Oh, Ellie, you and your team have really outdone yourselves this time. I hadn't seen these yet. Wow!" She looked at Michter and said, "Roger, which one did you choose? It must've been so difficult!"

Ellie cut in and answered, "He hates all of them."

"I didn't say that!" he objected.

"Actually, that was *exactly* what you said. 'Hate.' Oh, and then you followed up with the word, 'terrible.'"

In a sober and deliberate tone, Mill said, "You must be joking with my granddaughter, Mr. Michter, if she and her team say these are the ones, they've put in a lot of work designing them and testing them."

Michter tried to spool up the charm, "Please, call me 'Roger.'"

Not hearing him, Mill calmly let out a breath and said, "Well, I guess it will be easier for me to vote 'No' on the hotel later tonight if you don't have a logo. Gee, if you can't even pick a good logo out of eight great logos, I bet you can't get a hotel built."

"Grandma!" Ellie shouted.

Mill didn't hear her either, "What a shame." She gently shook her head looking downward.

"Grandma, do not try to coerce someone into picking one of our designs!"

"I'm sorry, dear. Did you say something?" Mill said as her iced tea was delivered.

Michter was a couple of seconds behind the conversation because he had just realized he may have taken very good aim at his own foot right before shooting it, "I'm sorry, Mill. Did you say, 'Vote, no?' Are *you* on the town council?"

With an Easter Sunday morning smile, Mill said, "Why, *Mister* Michter, did they not tell you? I am 'councilperson-at-large' for the village of Sounion. I've been on town council since Ellie here was in high school. It is part of what I do to help."

Michter looked like he just got slapped and repeated, "I'm sorry-I'm sorry, *you're* on town council?"

Not dulling a lumen from her smile, Mill said, "Of course, I am. No one told you that?"

"*You* never told me that! It was not on our town council list of names." Michter looked at Mill and then at Ellie in an accumulated accusation.

"*Mister* Michter—"

"Call me, *Roger*," there was a suggestion of panic.

"What do you think *at-large* means? I kind of fill in the gaps, but rest assured, I vote on every measure. It's my civic duty!"

"Grandma, stop it. I can fight my own battles."

"I'm sorry, dear. I'm having a little trouble hearing today," Mill said as she theatrically bent her ear.

"There is nothing wrong, and never has been wrong, with your hearing, Grandma."

Roger Michter's mind was racing. In a razor thin race to get the hotel approved, he needed every friend he could get and he'd just offhandedly offended a council member just hours before the vote. He tried to get back some lost ground, "I'm sure one of the logos will work out, eventually, just some small adjustments."

"You said, 'hate' a minute ago." Ellie said accusingly.

"I was overreacting! I'm under a lot of stress with the vote."

"I bet you are," murmured Mill.

Michter reached over and took the stack of logos from Mill. He looked at the first one in the stack and quickly said, "Yes-yes. This was my favorite. Mmmmmm. I really like the font you used and the color palette is sublime."

Ellie had heard enough. "Give me a break, Michter." She slapped both hands down on the table. It made all the glasses wobble as if they had vertigo. I'm sorry. I'm leaving." She got up, pulled some bills out of her jeans back pocket, counted out twenty-five dollars and threw it on the table. "Lunch is on me. Leave a big tip."

"Where are you going?!" Michter asked. He grabbed at her arm and Ellie shrugged him off like Walter Payton going into the end zone.

She said sardonically, "To work on some new logos, Mr. Michter."

"Please, call me, 'Roger!'" he said to her back as she walked out of the diner and left Michter and Mill there.

Chapter 21.

The vote

The vote to allow a luxury hotel to be put up in Sounion Cove was held that evening. Town council chambers were quite small so people started showing up two hours before the proceedings were to begin.

Mayor Archie Richardson was the last to arrive. All council members had gotten there early and were going through the crowd getting some feedback and each taking about two dozen questions before the vote.

Archie had a little mariner's bell from a salvaged 1825 shipwreck near Sounion that he used to call town council meetings to order. At exactly seven, he struck it gently three times. Its pitch perfectly pierced the commotion.

"If it's okay with everyone, could we take our seats, please? Let us dispense with the minutes to save time as debate may take quite a while."

Making his way into the chambers, as if the Red Sea were parting, came Beckwith Chambers. He looked like a million dollars (or maybe, a billion dollars) with a Saville Row-tailored jacket, an open-collar white silk shirt, smart-looking jeans and Armani sandals.

Ellie looked over to the other side of the room at the "hotel people" of Roger Michter, Morris Barkwell, and James Winnington III perusing intently at sheaths of paper as if Talmudic scholars.

Mill caught Ellie's eye, looked over to Chambers and back over to the hotel people, and mouthed the word, *"Surrounded,"* as she sat in the middle of the other council members.

Mayor Richardson began to speak and he was immediately cut off by Morris Barkwell, the attorney for the hotel, "Point of parliamentary procedure!" he yelled.

"Mr. Barkwell, we have not begun to even begin our proceedings tonight," the mayor said.

"The Sounion Hotel would like to reserve the right to speak first and give our final statements on the monetary and cultural benefits of the hotel."

"Mr. Barkwell, you'll be given plenty of time to speak."

"But as I understand it, you limit discussion to two minutes per person!"

Archie Richardson, not looking like the angry and frustrated man outside of Roger Michter's house when he was trying to abruptly leave, was calm, cool, and collected. The hotel people were on his turf now and he wasn't about to let them forget it. "We have provided extra time for you," he said like a pediatrician to a child who couldn't pick out which small figurine toy to take home after a visit.

Ellie noticed that Claude Morgan and his captain were both standing near the town council members implying that no one in the audience should get too far out of hand.

Debate began promptly at seven-twenty after Morris Barkwell, Roger Michter, and James Winnington III spoke. Ellie couldn't look at Winnington and not think about how he'd tried to bully her in the ladies room of the high school gym not that many days ago.

All-in-all, Ellie thought the hotel people's talk was brief and persuasive. As a coda, they turned the floor over to Beckwith Chambers, who for five minutes, in his smooth British accent eloquently explained how Sounion would have the best of both worlds: an unspoiled seaside village with a wonderful mostly out-of-way luxury hotel bringing added dollars, jobs, and panache.

Ellie noticed that Beckwith, though talking smooth, was sweating profusely and was quite pale by the end of his five minutes.

And the raucous debate started.

Nearly two hours later, and literally, two hours of two minutes at a time for each person who wanted to say something. The people of Sounion heard every angle of the pros and cons. From the NIMBY ("Not In My Backyard") folks to the yuppies who'd started to gentrify Sounion in the early parts of the decade that wanted to see a little more sophistication and spice added to the old world charm—and every angle in between.

The town council room was getting hotter and hotter, and not just emotionally, at the end of debate, people were fanning themselves as if at the Scopes Monkey Trial.

Ellie looked over and saw Mac the Pilot, with his omnipresent baseball cap on, come in right at the end of debate and stood not terribly far from Beckwith Chambers. He looked over at her and tipped his cap. She hadn't noticed before, but Jessica Traverts was in the crowd on the wall not far from Mac the Pilot and Beckwith Chambers. She was passing her business card to a couple of the yuppie women trying to drum up some catering gigs. She had her auburn hair pulled back in a ponytail and mixed in with the yuppie women seamlessly.

Archie, from his chair at the front spoke to Mac the Pilot. "Hey, Mac. You've never been to one of our meetings, but there is a strict *No hats inside* mandate that's been around since about the turn of the century."

Mac the Pilot chuckled and said, "You're kidding, right?"

"He is most certainly not kidding," said a woman on town council seated on the far right with her hair in a tight bun looking like a Dickens character and twenty years older than Mill.

Mac the Pilot shook his head and then dramatically took his cap off and bowed like Dumas' D'Artagnan to the elderly woman. No one was sure if they'd ever seen Mac the Pilot without that darn hat on. He was mostly bald with wisps of dark reddish-gray hair. Very Jimmy Buffett.

Remarkably, the room grew even hotter. Just as Mayor Richardson was about to call the roll for voting, Beckwith Chambers, who, by now looked like he'd jogged out to Sounion from Manhattan asked for a glass of water. "I'm burning up!" Several people jumped up and got him water from one of the vending machines.

The roll was taken for the vote. Mill was first and without hesitation voted "Yes" for the hotel. Half the people in the room gasped and the other half clapped in utter surprise. Ellie looked over at Roger Michter who was looking at Mill and putting his hand over his heart in a relieved gesture.

Ellie thought: *Grandma, if you did some deal for me...*

Other votes were casts by the council members and the tally went back and forth.

There was a surprise flipped vote by someone who everyone thought would vote for, but then voted against. More gasps as everyone realized that it was a tie vote.

And the room now moved its collective gaze toward Mayor Archie Richardson, the person, when needed, voted to break town council ties.

There was a Frank Capra-esque hush to the room as Archie began to speak, "Actually, I've been wondering all day if my vote would really even be necessary. In my informal polling of the council members, it's gone back and forth over the past several days." He paused a few seconds to let that sink in, and then held up an old oblong binder-like manuscript, "Has anyone read this? I mean really read it? This is the original village charter from when our founders started this wonderful village over one hundred and fifty years ago."

Morris Barkwell looked like he was about to spontaneously combust and burst into flames. He could smell a legal loophole a mile away and town council chambers had a pungent aroma in it right now. Richardson continued, "All of our laws are based on these. As a matter-of-fact, whenever we enact a law, or amend a law, it is *still* handwritten in here."

He flicked the pages almost reverently and went near the beginning, "And so I've been reading some of the original intents and conditions from our founders, and I came upon this very interesting, and very clear codicil from all those years ago." He cleared his throat and read slowly to the crowd, *"It is hereby decreed that Sounion Cove should be the kindest and most outgoing of all the fishing villages on Long Island, therefore, whenever a visitor shall come in by sea, or by land, that person or persons should only be housed and hosted by a family in this village and no Inn shall ever be erected in Sounion now and forever more. We are a friendly village."* He looked up from the binder and said, "And so, for this reason, I vote no."

And the entire room erupted.

In the middle of it was Mayor Archie Richardson, grinning like the Cheshire Cat. He knew something was up with the hotel people, he couldn't put his finger on it, but he wanted to make sure the hotel people got out of his town.

Mill looked over to Archie Richardson and made a little bow of admiration, which he promptly returned.

"What?!" Beckwith Chambers exploded. "How *dare* you!" His skin was about as pale as snow and he was sweating bullets. His hands were shaking. He pushed a woman aside and stood up on her chair so everyone would see and hear him. He theatrically stretched his arms out wide and began, "I would like to say—"

That was all he got out as his eyes rolled to the back of his head and he tumbled off the chair and landed in a heap. There was complete silence and then pandemonium as everyone moved and crushed in around him.

Mac the Pilot used his big shoulders to move people out of the way, his hat now securely back on his head, as he moved toward Beckwith. Ellie moved in also.

Chambers had fallen in such a manner that his chest was on the floor and his head turned toward the door.

"Get out of the way, you idiots! He's in diabetic shock!" Mac yelled.

Mac the Pilot got to Chambers, flipped him over and roughly started going through his pockets. "He's probably dead already, but just maybe."

Mac the Pilot reached deep into Chambers' breast pocket and pulled out a two syringes wrapped in plastic. He fumbled with the wrapping on one of them, screwed the syringe on, pulled up Chambers' shirt exposing his stomach and then plunged the syringe into his stomach a few inches from belly button. It seemed like it took forever to get all the medicine in. After it was all in, Mac the Pilot, breathing heavily, sagged against the wall and said, "I hope I wasn't too late."

A moment later, in a voice as crystal clear as a Grand Teton morning, in the most precise American accent anyone had heard, Beckwith Chambers' opened his eyes and said plainly,

"This play is called *Our Town*. It is written by Thornton Wilder."

And he died.

Chapter 22.

Phone call to a longtime companion

Medics, Claude Morgan, and a resident doctor who just happened to be at the vote all tried to resuscitate him, but Beckwith Chambers was as dead as Julius Caesar.

A half hour later, and with three-quarters of the original crowd still there, several people were coming up to the crestfallen Mac the Pilot, patting him on the back or warmly shaking his hand and giving him several sincere *You did your bests* and *There was nothing you could've dones* and *It was his times.*

Claude Morgan and his police captain took several statements. Out of respect, Morgan let Mac the Pilot sit and rest, so he went last. All the hotel people gave statements. Jessica, who was about to have a nervous breakdown shakily signed her statement. Morris Barkwell and Roger Michter signed their name as if they were signing their death warrants.

Mac the Pilot gave his version of events. Morgan and his captain asked several questions, the only one Ellie heard was from Morgan:

[Morgan]: Thought we'd had some luck when you found the two insulin syringes in his breast pocket. You yelled out that he was in diabetic shock. How did you know that?

[Mac the Pilot]: I flew him out here. I usually carry a couple of Pepsis in a cooler and a bag of candy on the plane. I offered him one and he said he couldn't because he was diabetic.

It took another hour for everyone to leave. Morgan said he would advise next of kin and they would identify the body.

Morris Barkwell marched up and said, "I will identify the body. Officially, that is."

Morgan raised his eyebrows and asked, "Are you next of kin?"

"No, not really. However, I am lead counsel for the hotel, and he is our largest funder, I feel I should identify the body."

"You know you can't do that."

"Maybe if I file a motion with the court, they will hear me."

"Oh, you do just that," he said archly. "Meanwhile, I'll be contacting a *family* member."

Jessica called over to Mac the Pilot and asked meekly, "I hate to ask after all this, but can you help me tomorrow with a wine delivery? It's the biggest event of the summer. I forgot all about the shipping. I've been helping Roger with the presentations and forgot all about it."

He stared at her blankly for several moments. Jessica actually started to turn away thinking he wasn't going to answer. He nodded slightly and said a quiet, "Sure, whatever."

She gave him a big hug of thanks and a kiss on the cheek. Ellie wondered again if Jessica was involved with Mac as well.

Michter sidled up to Ellie, put her bicep in a vice lock and said through clenched teeth, "This isn't over. Just because we lost doesn't mean we're leaving. I want new logos ready by eleven tomorrow morning."

Claude Morgan saw the harshness of the squeeze out of the corner of his eye, but was unable to really do anything about it until Michter went up to him a few minutes later to thank him and say good night. He shook Morgan's hand, Ellie saw, but Morgan suddenly was the complete opposite of himself and became Mr. Talkative, all the while pumping Michter's hand—talking and talking about this and that. Ellie could now see Morgan was squeezing Michter's hand into sawdust in retaliation. Michter was trying to smile and not shriek. Ellie thought his molars might fall out, he was in so much pain.

Morgan let go eventually, smiled warmly, patted Michter gently on the shoulder, and lapsing into a little Quebecois said, *"Bonne nuit, à bientôt."*

Mill and Ellie walked slowly home. Neither knew what to think. Mill wondered aloud, "I wonder if Archie Richardson feels guilty about voting no and a person dying right after because of it."

"Knowing Archie, very much so."

"What did Michter say to you?"

"He wants more logo ideas; he says they're not pulling up stakes."

"Interesting. I wonder how many county, state, and federal injunctions Morris Barkwell is going to be filing overnight."

Ellie took off the cotton cardigan she was wearing to ward off the nighttime chill walking home. Under, she had on a sleeveless floral blouse. She showed Mill the bruising starting to form on her bicep where Michter grabbed her. Mill stopped in her tracks, turned purplish-crimson in the face and yelled at the top of her lungs, "Where is my shotgun?!"

She started jogging ahead of her granddaughter. Ellie asked, "What are you *doing*?"

Over her shoulder, she said, "I'm jogging ahead to get my shotgun, then I am getting in my car, driving to Roger Michter's house and turning his head into a canoe. What does it *look like* I'm doing?"

It took Ellie almost two football fields worth of running to catch up to Mill. They rounded the corner and made their way to Mill's driveway with Ellie all along repeating, "Please tell me you're kidding. Please tell me you're kidding."

"I never kid when my granddaughter has been injured."

Through serendipity, Claude Morgan's squad car was in Mill's driveway. He was leaning against it with something in his right hand. He kept dropping in his left hand. It looked like a short necklace or bracelet. He didn't say hello when they walked up, what he did say was, "Who is Jack Harper?"

Confounded, they both shrugged.

"I found this on the floor near Chambers."

He let it dangle from his hand and drop into Ellie's outstretched hand. It was a stainless steel bracelet with a thick red asterisk and a staff of Aesculapius symbol on it. It had an *In Case of Emergency* number, along with the type of diabetes (Type 2).

Morgan flipped it over. It read, "Jack Harper."

"Are you sure this came from Beckwith Chambers?"

He looked over at Mill and pointed at her with his chin. "Mill, you knew everyone at that meeting tonight, right?"

"Absolutely."

"Is there anyone in town named 'Jack Harper'?"

"No."

"I had radioed in the name as I was driving over here. There's no one on the tax rolls with that name. And, no outsider from another town comes over to Sounion town council meetings on a weekday night in the summer just for the fun of it. No member of the press was named Jack Harper."

"Do you mind if I go upstairs and use your phone?" he asked.

Concerned about the bug still in her phone, Ellie said, "Maybe use the phone in the big house, maybe a little more private if you know what I mean."

Morgan caught on, "I'm going to call this emergency number and see who answers."

The three of them went into the big house and Morgan called. The conversation went something like this as Ellie and Mill couldn't hear what was being said on the other end. Morgan repeated as much as he could.

"Hello? Sir, my name is Officer Claude Morgan of the Sounion Police Department out here on Long Island. I'm holding in my hand a diabetes bracelet for a 'Jack Harper.' Sir, could you describe Jack Harper to me?" [Pause as he listened.] "Understood. That matches a man we have out here. But, this man speaks with a British accent and goes by the name of Beckwith Chambers. He's a billionaire. Are you his father or brother, sir?" [Pause as he listened.] "Sir, I'm very sorry to tell you that Jack Harper died of diabetic shock about ninety minutes ago. He was at a town council meeting and got very upset and went into shock. Someone pulled an insulin syringe out of Chambers', uh, Harper's breast coat pocket and administered it, but it was too late." [Much longer pause as he listened.]

Morgan put his large hand over the mouthpiece, looked over to Ellie and Mill with a mournful face and said, "He's crying."

After several moments, Ellie heard plainly through the phone an angry, *"They got him, didn't they?"*

"Sir, could you tell me who 'they' are?" [Pause as he listened, then methodically repeated what was being said to him.] "His real name is Jack Harper and you are his longtime companion. You both live in Greenwich Village. Jack Harper is originally from Omaha, Nebraska. Jack Harper was a former Off-Broadway actor, who auditioned

for a 'role' to become this person Beckwith Chambers. A couple of people asked him to assume this role for a fee of $150,000 dollars a year including an apartment and expenses. He's been doing it for about five years. They initially told him that they were running a tax dodge through him, but over the past year or so, he thought they were doing something really nefarious—something that directly hurt other people. They created a whole person—literally created a billionaire though he didn't, nor did any of the bank accounts directly-related to Beckwith Chambers that he could draw from, have anything like that kind of money in them. They did create a British tax number and bribed someone in the U.K. tax offices to give the appearance he was a billionaire. All phony accounting. The U.K. government thinks he's legit. He was simply playing the part for the people who hired him. They did several press releases and photo opportunities a year at big events where he would donate money. Just to keep him "real." He was even on Page Six of the New York Post *with several Hollywood actresses. He essentially became this person about one week a month. The rest of the time, he lived quietly here in Greenwich Village. Living quietly was part of the agreement." [Pause again.]*

"He's crying again."

"Sir, did he ever give you someone's name? Was he getting scared?" [Pause.] "Oh, he was getting scared? They were putting a lot of pressure on him to really sell he was Beckwith Chambers, billionaire. [Pause.] Sir, what was the name of the person who would contact him? [Pause.] Say, that again. Are you saying 'Maurice' is the name . . . oh, 'Morris' is the name? Sir, by any chance, would that first and last name be 'Morris Barkwell' and is he a real estate attorney?" [Pause.] "Okay, thank you for confirming it is Morris Barkwell."

Ellie and Mill looked at each other. A cold chill ran up their spines.

"Sir, I'm sorry, what is your name? Ah, yes. Jerry Livingston. I am very, very sorry for your loss. It seems you two were very close and dear to one another. Listen, I'm going to call you later to help you make arrangements, okay?

And, perhaps you'll come out in the morning and identify the body." [A very long pause.] "I'm sorry, Jerry. Truly, I am. I'll call back within the hour and help get everything started for you. Goodbye for now."

He pulled out his walkie-talkie and said, "Cap? Come in, Cap. Yeah, can we find where Morris Barkwell is renting this week and bring him in for questioning? I've got an angle on our hotel people. Yes, sir. I'll be down at the station in five minutes, sir. I'm finishing up with some related questioning."

Ellie asked, "Morris Blackwell created a fictitious character called 'Beckwith Chambers' out of thin air?"

"It seems so," said Morgan.

"Why would he do that?"

"Tax dodge?"

Mill said out loud, "You can create a tax dodge a lot of different ways without creating a fictitious human being."

Ellie asked, "Why would a group of hotel people create a fictitious person?" She started walking up the garage stairs to her room. She stopped halfway, turned and, as she began nodding her head said, "I think I may be going crazy, but I think I'm starting to figure some things out."

"What kind of things?" Morgan asked.

"Let me think. And I need another question answered that's bothering me." She waved goodnight to them both, walked up the rest of the stairs, and closed the door to her room.

Chapter 23.

Drawing

Knowing that her phone was still bugged, she called Bobby her assistant from Mill's phone in the main house. "Bobby, I know it's late, but could you do another huge favor for me? Your brother, the FBI guy, could you ask him a question? If someone wanted to smuggle not a vast quantity but several dozen pounds, say, a week, of cocaine or heroin, and it was flown in, where would it come from? Specifically, would it come from somewhere with pink beaches?"

Bobby said he'd call back in ten minutes with everything she'd need to know. It seemed Bobby's brother slept less than Bobby did.

She went back up to her room and pulled out her sketch book, she flipped to the page she'd done a few days ago—it seemed like forever ago—where she'd drawn little icons of the people she'd met when she got to Sounion for Memorial Day weekend.

Horizontally-aligned across the sketch pad page were: *James Winnington III. Ripped Jeans. Skewed Hat. Roger Michter. Jessica Traverts. Morris Barkwell. Mac the Pilot. Claude Morgan. Beckwith Chambers.*

Above each name, she had sketched a little icon.

Above *Ripped Jeans*, she had drawn a tombstone with an "RIP" on it.

Above *James Winnington III*, she had drawn the vest of a three-piece suit.

Above *Skewed Hat*, she had drawn the skewed hat he wore at the town meeting with the logo she'd designed on it. She now added a tombstone under the hat similar to the *Ripped Jeans* tombstone with a little "RIP" on it.

Above *Roger Michter*, she had drawn a hotel.

Above *Jessica Traverts*, she had drawn several hearts with an extending cupid arrow to *Roger Michter*. She now amended that icon to also point an arrow to *James Winnington III*. She stared at the page for a few minutes.

Then drew a *dotted* line to *Mac the Pilot* and added a question mark.

Above *Morris Barkwell*, she had drawn a law book with two bloodsucking fangs going into it.

Above *Mac the Pilot*, she had drawn a seaplane with pontoons and little waves. She put a baseball cap on top of the seaplane because of his omnipresent hat.

Above *Claude Morgan*, she had drawn a police hat.

Above *Beckwith Chambers*, she had drawn a Union Jack. She now appended */ Jack Harper* to the original name and drew a thick asterisk and a staff of Aesculapius symbol from the diabetes bracelet. He got an RIP tombstone as well. She drew a dotted line from Morris Barkwell to him.

Mill shouted up from the driveway that the phone in the main house was for her. She walked over quickly and picked up. It was Bobby. "He says it's The Bahamas. He says they've busted some smuggling there, but the FBI and DEA are so concentrated on the pipeline up from Central America, they haven't gotten over there as much as they want."

"Thanks, Bobby." And she hung up.

She went back to her room and began drawing new logos for *Sounion-by-the-Sea*. The concepts came fast and furious. She couldn't keep them away even if she wanted to. Ellie Pincrest was riled up. No one criticizes her firm's logos. Nobody. Roger Michter was going to see so many logos he liked, he wasn't going to know what to do with himself—and that was going to be the least of his problems.

She had several concepts she really liked, then called Michter. She guessed he'd still be seething from the *No* vote earlier that evening and that he would be up. He also had a much younger girlfriend. "Well, what do *you* want?" he said when she said hello. All of his previous charm and obsequiousness had melted away. Ellie wondered if he was the mastermind of this and not Barkwell or Winnington. With Barkwell's hand now exposed as the creator of Beckwith Chambers, née Jack Harper, Michter would have to be reeling, right?

She then thought Michter may not know about Beckwith Chambers' real identity at all.

"I have some new concepts I think you'll like. I want to see you first thing in the morning."

He paused for a moment. "You're sure they're good? I didn't like the last ones."

"They're quite good. Can we say ten tomorrow morning?"

"Of course. It will be just me and Winnington. Nobody can find Morris Barkwell."

Ellie held her tongue, but was thinking, *I bet!* She did say out loud, "I'm sorry about Beckwith. He seemed like a very good person."

"Yes, the best. He will be deeply missed," Ellie was surprised by the sincerity in his voice.

Ellie pushed her luck. "Will the funding be hurt with his death?"

Michter was offended by the question, "No, it's written into our agreements, even in the case of death. Beckwith was always very keen about those kinds of things. He used to say he was accustomed to 'the tyranny of small details.'"

"Well, goodnight. See you early tomorrow."

"Bye," Michter said curtly.

The concept she focused on most was one the firm had decided against back in Manhattan, a sketch Ellie had done very early in the process, that of a seaplane. The seaplane dock wasn't far from the where the hotel would be and Manhattanites would be flying out here in droves. It was the thing most unique about the hotel. Everyone in Manhattan would be talking about the cachet of *You know, the smart way out there is just to take the seaplane from the East River.*

Drawing and refining, applying different angles to the plane, something of a retro look.

Something was nagging at her.

It seemed like it had been nagging her for several days. It was drilling into her psyche.

She stared at the sketched planes, she'd even done one in perspective over water with moonlight behind it and then a thought engulfed her. *"God Almighty,"* she said out loud. And her hands began to shake uncontrollably. She dropped her sketch pencil. It took her three tries to pick it up. It was like her fingers had stopped working.

She put her head in her hands.

It took her almost a half hour to calm down.

Claude Morgan picked up phone on a call from Ellie. Instead of saying hello, he tried to be funny, "So you're calling me on the rebound from your ex?"

She was calmed down enough that she gave a feint chuckle, "Actually, I do want to see you, and no, not for sex. Besides, you don't seem like the kind of guy who'd want to be with a girl on the rebound."

"Rebound girls are like KGB cars, they don't necessarily take you where you want to go."

"Seriously, would you mind coming over?"

"Leaving now, see you in a few minutes," he said.

Morgan was there in eight minutes. The squad car pulling in woke Mill up and she went out of the main house and up to Ellie's room as well.

Ellie started with her first theory and explained it.

Then said her second theory and explained that as well.

Then her third, coupled with a proposal that she would give all of the hotel people her theories at Michter's when she showed the logos in the morning.

Mill about fell over.

"You're crazy if you think I'm going to let you go over there tomorrow with no back-up," Morgan said to her.

"You can be there, but just come maybe ten minutes later; park your car down the road and walk up."

"These people kill people."

"If they think it will be anything but a simple logo presentation, they'll think there's nothing to suspect. They just see me as the nothing logo designer. Ten tomorrow morning?"

"Ten tomorrow morning," he said.

"I'll drive," said Mill.

Chapter 24.

The Final Chapter: The Presentation

Ellie didn't sleep that night. She spent every moment possible refining the logos. She was going to make this seem as real as possible. She also spent considerable time rehearsing what she was going to say to the group and end this.

A little after five in the morning, the Sun glowed and broke over the horizon in a pink that was almost fluorescent. A sobering thought occurred to her and she said it out loud to the horizon, "Is this the last sunrise I'm ever going to see?"

She tried to suppress the thought with reminding herself that Morgan would be there with his captain, eventually. She wondered if the ten-minute delay was a good idea and decided not to dwell too much on it.

Mill made Ellie breakfast around eight and they talked about Ellie's theories about the hotel group. "What if you're flat wrong? That you've thought it all through and you're just *wrong?* You've got plenty of conjecture and a lot of leaps of faith, especially with regard to the deaths of *Ripped Jeans* and *Skewed Hat*. How Beckwith Chambers died has more than just a couple of *what ifs* in it."

"Then I'll be in a whole lot of trouble. So much trouble I'll have to resign from the firm, have no life—never get a job in design again, and I'll likely be sued for every cent I have and then some. I'll have to file for bankruptcy." She gave a wan smile, "Maybe filing for bankruptcy will make me forget Stephen."

Mill snapped her fingers indicating a swell idea and said, "Maybe you could have Stephen's new wife, the *Playboy* centerfold lawyer, defend you if you get sued for slander. Or maybe her expertise is in bankruptcy."

Ellie laughed and threw a strip of bacon at her grandmother's head.

"Too soon?" Mill said with a quizzical look as she plucked the bacon stuck to her silver hair.

Ellie went back up to her room to do one more thing before Mill drove her over to Michter's beach house: She wrote out her will.

Ellie Pincrest didn't have many worldly possessions. She had a comfortable co-op she'd recently bought, a string of pearls her mother bought her upon her graduation, several pieces of jazz royalty memorabilia that someone would find valuable, the Warhol. All of her friends were married, most had children and lived in Westchester or some other suburb. Those friendships had faded over the past few years. Too little time on both sides of the equation. A little tear came to her eye when she thought that not many would miss her for long. Mill would certainly. Her mother would be blue, hopefully, but Ellie thought her mother would simply drown herself in work at the emergency room. Her father would do the same and go back on tour. Stephen, her ex, would say "Oh, that's a darn shame," and Ellie would end up a smile on his face his wife would never understand.

She was a grinder. She knew that. She cared about her work and her work had rewarded her by placing her at the top of the mountain in the most competitive design environment on the planet. She shook her head and said, "No, regrets," softly as she signed her will with her distinctive signature.

Getting up from the writing table, she straightened herself and said more clearly, "Taking yourself a little seriously this morning, eh, girl? You're not Gary Cooper in *High Noon*."

Mill already had the car running and the passenger door open when Ellie made her way down the stairs. She noticed there was a long thick beach blanket in the space behind the seats. "What's the beach blanket for?"

Mill acted surprised, "Hmph, what beach blanket?"

Claude Morgan and his police captain were in the driveway as well. The captain spoke first, "You better know what you're doing. I'm all for thinking out of the box for solving crime—especially one this big—and even plausible deniability, but I'll be out of a job before lunch if this thing goes tapioca."

"I think I have this all figured out."

"I'd like for you to be safe. I can give you a small caliber gun you can put in the back of your jeans. Your blouse will hide it."

"I'd likely shoot one or both butt cheeks off," she said.

With the tense atmosphere, the captain tried not to laugh but couldn't. He became serious again, "If I hear one peep from that beach house, Claude and I are going in there with extreme malice."

"I shouldn't be at too much risk in there," she said with too much hopefulness in her voice.

"You already *are* at risk!" Morgan yelled. The more Morgan thought about it as he tossed and turned overnight, the more he didn't like the plan, no matter how well Ellie believed she had thought it out.

The captain went up, held Ellie by the shoulders and said quietly, "I used to be in SWAT in the city. Happens. Bad things happen to good people, okay? I've seen very well-intentioned good people who absolutely knew it was better for them to go in first before the police to talk to the person they knew-oh-so-well in a tense situation, get shot in the face for no good reason other than they were just trying to help."

"I'll be alright. The murderer of three people will be there and I know who it is."

"And you're not telling us exactly who that is, right? You've left that person out of your theories."

"Revealing the murderer will reveal all the players and their roles. The more I think about it, it's like chess pieces moving across the board. Even the pawn. And there's definitely a pawn at play here. I've got to move the pawn first. The first move makes other moves happen. Some of my conjecture needs to be filled in by them. And, of course, I could be completely wrong. If that's what ends up happening, I'll need to find a very big rock to hide under."

The captain said, "I'd like to have this done with no Feds dropping five attack helicopters on the house."

From the driver's seat of the Karmann Ghia, Mill added, "And I'd like to not turn Sounion into a news sensation. That last time we had big news here, Charles Lindberg stayed at a beach house for the month of August. That's the kind of news we like. Nothing news. I don't want the news and lore to be *Sounion Shoot-Out* for the next fifty years."

"You two hang back about five or ten minutes, then come quietly into the driveway," Ellie said again.

"We plan on parking about two hundred yards down the beach road, hoofing it, and quietly entering the house."

"Don't be too early." She paused, "And for heaven's sake, don't be too late."

Mill and Ellie left and drove over to the beach road and down. About a quarter mile from Michter's house, they saw Jessica Traverts jogging down the road toward the house with a comely spandex pink top, black running shorts and lemon yellow Nike running shoes. Jessica saw them, gave them a big smile and waved.

Mill said, "Wow, you're off to a good start. Good call on not having the police be right with us. Jessica's first question out loud to everybody would be 'Say, what are those two policemen doing in the driveway?'"

They pulled into the sweeping driveway at Michter's. Ellie could see through the mostly glass house and pulled up near the beach—and not at the dock closer to downtown—was Mac the Pilot's plane. He was unloading Jessica's wine cases from his seaplane.

"Stay here," Ellie said.

Mill looked at her granddaughter, "One hair on your head gets hurt and they better hope the police get them first, because I will do unspeakable things to them."

"If this goes badly and I don't come out on my own two feet, tell Mom and Dad that I love them."

Ellie leaned over and gave her grandmother a kiss on the cheek, got out of the car, and up the walkway to the front door.

Roger Michter opened the door and was disappointed to see Ellie there. "I was hoping it would be Morris Barkwell."

"I don't think he'll be coming today," Ellie said.

"What does that mean?"

She was spared an explanation by Jessica finishing her run and bounding up the walkway and through the door. She gave Roger a little peck and he brightened.

Roger said to Ellie, "These better be good."

"They're quite good."

He showed her in and led her to the big dining table near the enormous open glass window doors that looked out on to the beach and Mac the Pilot's plane. Jessica was getting herself a glass of water. James Winnington III was already at the table waiting for them.

Winnington offered her a glass of water, but Ellie was taking no chances on being drugged, so she declined even though her mouth was arid with nerves.

Mac the Pilot came in with the last of the wine cases, put them down, wiped his brow, and said, "Okay, Jessica, you're ready for tonight's party."

"Thanks!" Jessica said brightly from the kitchen sink.

Mac the Pilot took a seat on a chaise lounge on the patio just a few feet from where Ellie was presenting. "I'm bushed," he said as he cracked open a Budweiser. It was a little after ten, but he'd been working hard and probably up since the Sun rose.

Ellie began her presentation of a dozen new logos. She saved a special one for last. Michter was intently looking at them, nodding his head and smiling. He was talking about several ways he would approach the town council again to get the hotel approved. He was positive that Morris Barkwell was filing some air tight injunction somewhere—that's why he wasn't here yet—if only he would call in. He made several notes. He even jotted down some financial figures. Winnington barely looked at the logos, he couldn't keep his eyes off the shapely body of Jessica Traverts. She clandestinely blew him a kiss that he caught.

Michter was impressed with all the logos and was very enthusiastic about them. And then Ellie came to the last logo. "And I've got one very special logo to conclude my presentation and it comes with a few questions."

Michter cooed a little in anticipation, "Bring it on!"

She turned over the last of the logos as she saw Jessica walk from the kitchen and sit on another chaise not far from Mac.

The final logo featured a seaplane on a dark blue background with white "SOUNION BY THE SEA" in a circle around a seaplane that Ellie had intentionally put in pink.

Michter loved it. "Wow! It's so out of the box. I love how you married the dark blue background with the pink. It's so offbeat I'm sure it will be a hit. But, I have to ask, why did you choose pink for the plane? No one would ever be that bold."

In a clear voice that would reach the patio, Ellie made her opening chess move, "Because of the pink sand in Mac's plane."

From the patio, Mac slowly turned around and didn't give quite a menacing look, but it was clearly a look demanding caution. He got up, took off his omnipresent hat for a moment, smoothed the sweat off of his head and asked. "What's that about pink sand?"

Michter crowded in, "Oh, it's nothing-nothing. She used something she saw somewhere and used it in a design."

"There's no pink sand in *my* plane. There's never been pink sand *ever* in my plane," he said threateningly.

Ellie went for it. "It's pink sand from a beach somewhere in The Bahamas."

And James Winnington III stood up very quickly from the table. He didn't say anything, he just started breathing heavily.

Roger Michter stayed seated, confused, and asked Winnington, "The heck's wrong with you? Why are you breathing so hard?"

Jessica Traverts got up with a peculiar look on her face.

Ellie stared at Mac the Pilot and in a calm voice said, "You killed them. Didn't you?"

Roger Michter got up and with calming hands said, "Whoa-whoa. That's quite an accusation. If Morris were here, he'd have already threatened slander." He paused and then asked, "Killed *who*?"

Ellie didn't stop. She'd been rehearsing all night. She was either going to be dead in a few minutes, flat broke for the rest of her life, or these people were going to implode on themselves. She pointed her chin at Mac, "Something happened with those two who were killed: *Ripped Jeans* and *Skewed Hat*. They'd offended you in some way—or made you feel very unsafe. What was it, Mac? What did they do to you?

It kept bothering me, *Why would Mac the Pilot need to kill two people?* I couldn't get it out of my mind."

In an even voice, Mac the Pilot said, "I've killed no one. Those two *drowned.*"

"How did you know the second one drowned? As far as anyone knows, save for the coroner and the police, he died of a drug overdose."

"Guess I'm mistaken," he said flatly. His eyes were throwing daggers.

Undeterred, Ellie said, "Oh, let's not stop at those two, I know about you killing Beckwith Chambers as well."

"That is *enough!* We all saw he died of diabetic shock!" bellowed Michter. "For heaven's sake, more than half the town saw him die! Ms. Pincrest, are you feeling okay? Are you having some kind of mental breakdown?"

Michter's statements and questions stood in danger of being ignored. Ellie pressed on like a Math professor solving for *x*. "How do two people drown, a couple of days apart in exactly the same way?"

Mac the Pilot wasn't backing down in the slightest. "They just drowned. Or they were drunk or high or whatever and just swam out too far. Happens almost every week on the shores of Long Island. What? You think I grabbed them, frog marched them down to the water and stuck their head under? Those two weren't exactly weaklings and I'm not exactly a young man."

"Sure, sure," Ellie said agreeably. "But, how do you account for the trauma injuries? The coroner and police said it was like they'd been hit by a whale."

"Huh, maybe there's an angry whale off Long Island. You know they migrate past here all the time," Mac said.

Ellie pointed her chin at Mac again and quietly said, "You made them jump, didn't you?"

"My God," said Michter astonished.

"You promised them a ride home or to some hot spot or maybe just a joyride at night and you pulled a gun on them up in the airplane and said something like, 'I'll give you a sporting chance, I'll go down to two-hundred feet and you can jump instead of shooting you.' And they both took their chances, but you knew that a plane going a hundred and fifty miles an hour at two-hundred feet would stun them so badly or knock them out, they'd drown. Oh, and you made sure they were just close enough to shore to think they'd make it. When *Skewed Hat* showed up in the park with a cocaine needle in him, but he had *drowned*, I knew something crazy was happening here. You actually fished him out—dead!—and took that poor boy and stuck him in the park to humiliate him. The drug needle—disgusting. His hat must've blown off and stayed inside your plane when he opened the door, didn't it? That was a nice break for you. You could put it back on his head after he was dead. The rain was also a nice break for you. You were arrogant when you put him in the park, Mac. Both of those boys were desperate. No one can survive a close range bullet. And you knew a bullet could possibly be traced back to you, especially after Claude Morgan would run forensics."

"You've got an active imagination," the venom was pronounced now.

"And I know *why* you killed them both."

But Michter was absorbing enough to ask questions and cut her off. "What was that you said about Beckwith?"

"You mean Jack Harper?" she said.

"Who?" he was genuinely mystified which confirmed to Ellie that Roger Michter was the pawn in all of this. Along with three dead people.

"Beckwith Chambers is a canard."

"A what?" asked Michter.

"He's a lie. The idea was to create a billionaire who appeared to be funding your real estate deals, but I can assure you, Beckwith Chambers is really Jack Harper, a retired actor living—was living—in Greenwich Village with his longtime companion. Someone in this room gave Morris Barkwell orders to create this fake person to hide where your money really comes from."

Michter looked like he'd swallowed a squid, whole. "Tell me about his death first. That's what I care about."

She looked back over to Mac and narrowed her eyes. "The insulin."

Mac threw up his hands and yelled, "Oh, you've got to be kidding me! I almost saved his life!"

"No, you killed him. It's likely he'd have been okay if you wouldn't have done anything, but I remembered during your statement to Officer Morgan you'd offered him something from your candy bag and a Pepsi when you first met him on your plane. You offer that to everyone. You offer it to me when I fly with you. You said he turned you down because he was diabetic. That's when you got an idea. There was going to be some kind of event where he was going to need insulin, some emergency. And you were going to take care of him."

"And now I'm a doctor that knows everything about insulin and diabetes?"

"You're no doctor, but you *are* a thief. You knew enough that a massive dose would kill him. That's why you broke into the pharmacy the other night and made it look like it was a couple of juveniles. When Claude Morgan mentioned that kids had broken into the pharmacy, I thought it was odd. You never hear about pharmacies getting ransacked; then I started putting things together. When the inventory comes back of what was stolen, it will show the largest dosage syringe of insulin is missing and whatever teen smokescreen you created by stealing junk they would want. You trashed the place as well to make sure it confused the police."

"Wow, I thought I was a humble seaplane pilot, but you've got me as a doctor, a murderer, and a thief. What's next? Centerfielder for the Yankees?"

Ellie wasn't listening. She was so full of adrenaline her hands palsied a little. She was trying to remember the script. "When he passed out, afterwards, I thought it was interesting that you immediately said, 'He's in diabetic shock' and nothing like, 'He's having a heart attack' or epilepsy or heat stroke because it was a thousand degrees in council chambers that night or anything. You were ultra-specific."

"I was just lucky."

"Luck had nothing to do with it. This was planned and you were waiting for the right moment. You'd been carrying the syringe around with you. I bet the original plan was to plunge it into him the next time he rode your plane back to

Manhattan and tell the authorities 'He just died in my plane!'" Instead, he stayed out here. And you needed a roomful of witnesses. You hid the big syringe in your hand as you made your way over to him and then you pulled out two syringes from his breast pocket, his and the one you'd stolen from the pharmacy. You acted like you opened *his* syringe. What you really did was take the syringe *you* stole with the huge dosage, carefully assembled it in front of everyone to see, and dosed him, killing him. Everyone around would think he just carried an extra syringe and no one could see how big a dosage it was in all the confusion."

Michter spoke up. He was equal parts unbelieving and accusing, "Maybe he thought if one syringe broke, he could use the other. Why kill them? Why kill three people? Why kill Beckwith Chambers?"

"Officer Morgan spoke to his longtime companion. Harper, the fake Chambers, had started asking questions and he was starting to get scared as well. He knew something was up. I'm guessing the gunshot was meant for him and not Archie Richardson at the Memorial Day parade. The person in charge wanted to make sure that Harper/Chambers was playing his part. He was under enormous pressure to play his role. I'm also guessing that Archie Richardson really did think that gunshot was meant for him to warn him to get other council members to vote for the hotel, and at the very least, to break the tie. Two birds with one stone if you don't mind the cliché."

Mac the Pilot wasn't having any more of this, from the back of his trousers, he produced a thirty-eight caliber handgun and grabbed Jessica Traverts as a hostage. He stuck the gun into her temple. She screamed and began shaking uncontrollably.

Claude Morgan and his captain came through the door and ran to the back with their weapons out. "Drop it!" yelled Morgan.

"I'm taking my hostage and getting out of here!"

Ellie said something only two other people in the room understood, "Go ahead. *Shoot her.*"

Michter, Winnington, Morgan and the captain at the same time yelled, "Don't!"

"Go ahead," she said to Mac like she was offering him to go through a door in front of her.

Mac the Pilot screwed the muzzle of the thirty-eight into Jessica's temple. "Cops! Put down your weapons or I'll spray her brains all over the wall. Do it!"

"He won't do it," Ellie said with a rueful smile on her face.

Morgan yelled, "Ellie! This is serious situation! Why are you saying that?!"

You could hear small waves rhythmically hitting the pontoons of the seaplane.

"Because she's his daughter," she said.

As an astonished reflex for being found out, Mac the Pilot moved the gun away from Jessica's temple, but still had it aimed at her. Ellie kept filling in the blanks, "Because *Jessica Traverts* is the person running the entire enterprise. Because Jessica Traverts is the one who told Morris Barkwell to create a fake person, someone who could be passed off as a billionaire, and have a matching shell company that *Morris Barkwell* could write checks from. It's Jessica Traverts who is pulling everybody's strings all the while acting like an invisible caterer. She hid in plain sight."

She paused again and looked at Jessica and said slowly, "Because Jessica Traverts figured out that *Ripped Jeans* and *Skewed Hat* were plotting with James Winnington III against her."

"Plotting what?" Michter asked pleadingly.

"Jessica Traverts runs a massive cocaine and heroin operation and masks it and does distribution through her catering business. I was wondering why I didn't recognize many people at your party in Sounion. She launders the money through Beckwith Chambers as a shell company to your real estate investments, Roger. Chambers/Harper only saw a salary; he never touched any of the money. I don't know if Jessica runs money through anything else, but she definitely cleans her drug money through you. I couldn't begin to understand Morris Barkwell's legal and accounting mumbo-jumbo on setting it up and sustaining it, but the authorities sure will have someone who can."

Michter slumped down in his chair. He looked like he wouldn't mind if Mac the Pilot or the police shot him at this moment. "Drugs? How?" he mumbled out dejectedly.

Ellie pointed over to the wine case. "She transports them, with the help of her father, a pilot. She gets the drugs in the wine cases up from the Bahamas and he runs them up here." Ellie paused. "And the money is laundered through your real estate deals. Actually, your hotels are so successful, you've both laundered and made her even more money. For a while, I thought you were the mastermind because you are so successful at growing money for you and your investors, but then I figured out that Jessica's father is Mac the Pilot and tied them together."

"When she's dead, you won't feel so smart." Mac blurted.

Ellie poured it on. "The red hair. Mac's hair is mostly gray, but some red-auburn, just like Jessica's. I had never seen you with your hat off. Ever, in all these years. There was just enough auburn for a connection." She paused and then said, "And, they're both left handed."

"How do you know that?" Mac slipped.

"You both signed your police statements with your left hand."

Claude responded skeptically, "C'mon Ellie, that doesn't mean the kid will be left-handed."

She replied calmly without taking her eyes off of Jessica. "There's a southpaw in my office. She once told me that if *one* parent is left-handed, there's a one in four chance that the child will be left-handed. And besides, I noticed that every time there was a wine case around, Mac *and* Jessica were near it.

Michter cried out, "Go back to Beckwith. I don't understand. He was in the press all the time. His wire transfers for funding came in like clockwork. He's been my best financial backer in the quarter century I've done real estate! Are you telling me *he* was in on this as well?"

"No, not really. He was just playing a role. He didn't know about the drugs. He thought it was a fancy tax dodge—that's what Morris Barkwell told him—and he reasoned that was fine, especially for an aging unemployed rarely seen off-

Broadway actor. Nice salary, apartment in the Village, extremely comfortable lifestyle."

The news that Beckwith Chambers wasn't in on the drug operation gave Michter a tiny sliver of hope. "I always liked him. But in the end, he was just lying to me the entire time." His hope quickly landed like a thud.

Ellie said, "I'm sure that because of the nefarious nature of where the money was coming from, creating this fake person, this *illusion*, along with a dummy company they set up, everything appeared very copacetic. It must've been very hard keeping Beckwith Chambers' true identity a secret from you."

"What about Winnington?" Michter asked looking at him.

"On the money side of things, obviously, it was Jessica, Morris Barkwell, *and James Winnington*," Ellie said.

"You can leave me out of your little fairy tale, right now!" yelled Winnington as he thumped the table.

There was a tense quiet in the room. The police certainly had no intention of putting down their weapons, and Mac seemed equally averse to doing the same.

And for the first time, Jessica Traverts spoke.

The ersatz terror was gone. She spoke with a sinister lilt at James Winnington III, surreal as it was because her father still had a gun pointed at her head. "I had to keep my eye on you, James. I knew you were trying to backstab me and takeover my little importing business. So I let you into my bed."

A limp Winnington simply croaked out a, "No."

Then it was Michter's turn as he processed her words, "Darling! No!"

Traverts, now the puppet master, smiled at her older lover, "Sorry, Roger. It was just business. I needed to clean my money and real estate is the best way to do it. Morris and I scripted exactly what Beckwith was to say to you each time you two spoke. That's why Morris instructed him to be cryptic. Less risk. And anything odd he would say would be chalked up to the eccentricity of a billionaire. Roger, it's been almost five years together. It was a good run, now I'll have to clean my money in a new way." She shrugged as if she was discussing her laundry detergent preference.

"We were going to be married!" Michter protested.

Jessica Traverts tuned him out and she turned her attention back to Winnington who now was taking a few steps backward, even though Jessica was on the other side of the room. He was genuinely frightened of this woman. "James, you were naughty. You and I created something very smart. I put you into this at the ground floor. Made you loads of money—and yet, you still weren't satisfied. You, as an investment banker, needed to put funding with a business. That's what you do. So I created Beckwith Chambers along with Morris. We let you in on that as well. But you're smart, aren't you James? You started asking—how does Ms. Pincrest refer to them?—*Ripped Jeans* and *Skewed Hat* considerably more operational details. I'm guessing you were offering considerably higher cuts of the profits than I was giving them. The nitty gritty details that both of them took care of for me for distribution at the parties. So I started sleeping with you so I could find out what you knew. I would rummage around in your briefcase when you fell asleep after sex. And then, you naughty, you started asking my father even more questions." She crossed her arms and pouted, mocking him, "But you didn't know he was my father, now did you? After all this time, I never let that on, now did I?"

James Winnington III, all confidence, swagger, and bluster just a few days ago, was opening and closing his mouth, not able to speak. He very probably wasn't remembering to breathe either.

Ellie answered by mildly asking him a question. "James, Mac the Pilot offered you a ride back to Manhattan tonight, didn't he?"

He leaned over and steadied himself on the big table and finally answered in a whisper, "My God, I would've been next to jump out of the plane. Maybe I should've had bugged Jessica's phone instead of yours."

Jessica Traverts smiled in confirmation. "And just so you know, Ms. Pincrest, I helped fish *Skewed Hat* out of the water after my father made him jump. Thought he could betray me. The fool." She was very proud of herself. She had fooled everyone. *Almost.*

"Where's Morris Barkwell? He set up the Beckwith Chambers angle." Ellie asked Jessica.

"He's taken off. Sincerely, I don't know where he is. I'm sure he's set up some residence outside U.S. jurisdiction. He's a genius. The same way I'm about to take off and nobody will know where I am." She looked out at the seaplane and back to the group, "You didn't think I wouldn't have a contingency plan featuring a brand new identity for my father and I and twenty million dollars in a new bank account? Oh, and a pilot father to fly us there?"

While everyone was fixated on Jessica, Mac the Pilot took out a military-grade smoke bomb and threw it into the middle of the room. Because it was military-grade, it filled the room with smoke before it hit the floor. To embellish his point that he really wanted to escape with his daughter, Mac started firing his weapon.

Mac and Jessica, standing next to the big glass doors, must have slammed it shut and locked it on their way out. Jessica, who'd bolted for the front door instead of going blind and asphyxiated, heard at least two people hit the glass doors and bounce back. She was guessing it was Winnington and Michter.

Claude and the captain also went for the front door instead, and sprinted to circle around the side of the house and stop Mac the Pilot before he took off.

Before they got to the back of the beach house, Ellie heard a shotgun blast and her heart sank. She got around the corner and dashed toward the seaplane floating a few yards off the beach. Ellie saw Mac the Pilot writhing and rolling in pain on the beach clutching at his left arm. Jessica, astonished, frozen like a captured ice sculpture, had her hands raised. Five yards from them stood Mill with her shotgun, carefully hidden earlier under the beach blanket, the one she'd boisterously promised after Michter had bruised Ellie's arm.

Mill was growling. "Missy, I don't know who you are, but I mostly missed your father because I was running on sand with my little *blunderbuss* here. Oh, have you never heard that term? It's Dutch for *Thunder Pipe*, my late husband gave me this shotgun on our thirtieth wedding anniversary. I'm a terrible shot, but with that blast radius, I don't really need to be that accurate, now do I?"

Mac's arm was bleeding profusely and he'd have a very sore arm while serving out his jail time, which likely would be for the rest of his life and then some.

Claude and the captain took Jessica, Mac, and Winnington into custody for a variety of charges too long to list out. Michter's run in the real estate business had come to a screeching halt. The captain told Claude he'd, reluctantly, contact the Feds about Morris Barkwell so they could chase him down. He didn't like dealing with the Feds, but Morris was going to spend a long spell time in a Federal penitentiary as well.

The captain would give them the whole story, but at least a trial and the big takedown would not be in the evening news and papers keeping Sounion, the nice little fishing village that time had mostly forgot, exactly that way.

The End.

Stay tuned for the next Ellie Pincrest mystery, Missing in Manhattan.

Printed in Great Britain
by Amazon